W9-BUV-856

Also by Patrick Carman in Large Print:

Beyond the Valley of Thorns
The Dark Hills Divide

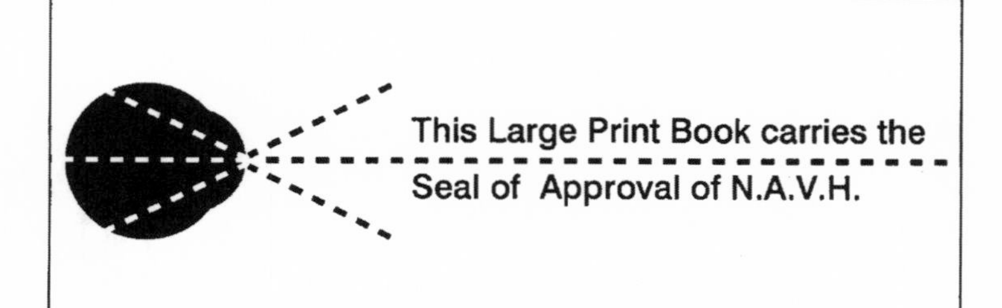

THE LAND OF ELYON BOOK 3

THE TENTH CITY

PATRICK CARMAN

Thorndike Press • Waterville, Maine

Recommended for Middle Readers

The Land of Elyon Book #3

Published in 2006 by arrangement with Scholastic, Inc.

Thorndike Press® Large Print The Literacy Bridge.

The tree indicium is a trademark of Thorndike Press.

The text of this Large Print edition is unabridged.
Other aspects of the book may vary from the original edition.

Set in 16 pt. Plantin.

Printed in the United States on permanent paper.

Library of Congress Cataloging-in-Publication Data

Carman, Patrick.
The tenth city / by Patrick Carman.
p. cm. — (The Land of Elyon ; bk. 3)
Summary: Alexa reveals the origin of the Land of Elyon while defending it against the evil Abaddon and his sinister forces, with not only the last Jocasta at stake but also the nature of the land itself.
ISBN 0-7862-7789-0 (lg. print : hc : alk. paper)
1. Large type books. [1. Human-animal communication — Fiction. 2. Voyages and travel — Fiction. 3. Magic — Fiction. 4. Large type books.] I. Title. II. Series: Carman, Patrick. Land of Elyon ; bk. 3.
PZ7.C21694Ten 2006b
[Fic]—dc22 2006013102

For Reece

THE LAND OF ELYON
Mount Laythen
The Dark Tower
The Northern Kingdoms
The Tenth City
Ainsworth
Castalia
The Valley of Thorns
The City of Dogs
The Great Ravine
The Dark Hills
Lunenburg
The Sly Field
Bridewell
The Western Kingdom
Fenwick Forest
Lathbury
Mount Norwood
Turlock
The River Roland

Life can only be understood backwards;
but it must be lived forwards.

S. A. Kierkegaard

AN INTRODUCTION TO THE TENTH CITY

There are a few notes I would like to offer before getting on with what remains of this story. We've visited many places and met many characters together, and I would hate for readers to find themselves confused by the events to come. Here then are a few reminders to help you keep your wits about you as we make our way to the Tenth City.

The Tenth City begins only hours after *Beyond the Valley of Thorns* comes to a close, with Alexa and most of her friends escaping the Dark Tower. I say *most* because Yipes has been taken by the evil Victor Grindall and his ogres to Bridewell, the last remaining walled city in The Land of Elyon, where he is being held captive with little hope of rescue.

Meanwhile, Alexa is adrift on the Lonely

Sea in the *Warwick Beacon*, a boat captained by one Roland Warvold, the brother of Thomas Warvold. Along with Alexa, Roland, and Thomas are Odessa the wolf, Murphy the squirrel, Squire the hawk, Thomas's wife, Catherine Warvold (also known as Renny), Armon the giant, and Balmoral, the leader of the rebellion in Castalia, along for the ride at Thomas Warvold's request.

And what of Alexa's father, Pervis Kotcher, Thomas Warvold's son Nicolas, and the others? We shall see them again before this tale is told.

As our story begins once more, night has fallen on the open sea, and our dear Alexa Daley is about to awaken to a world she's never seen before, a world of water and cliffs.

Come with me now as we travel the Lonely Sea together in search of the Tenth City.

— Patrick Carman
Walla Walla, April 2005

PART 1

CHAPTER 1

DARKNESS FALLS ON THE LONELY SEA

"We've made good speed today. I can't remember when I've covered so many miles so quickly."

It was a voice in the darkness.

"It would appear that the winds on the Lonely Sea are helping us along. The question is: Who controls these winds, and where are they taking us?"

I was waking from a long slumber on the deck of the *Warwick Beacon* when I heard this voice, and it seemed as though I'd awakened into a world that contained no light. Night had set on the Lonely Sea; not one glimmer from a single star could overcome the thick mist above and around us.

"Do you think she has anything to do with the wind at our back?"

"My guess is she has everything to do

with it. She and the last stone are tied to each other in a way I don't understand. She's the one we must protect . . . even at the expense of all the others."

The voices were coming from the front of the ship, about twenty feet away. Listening to their words drift out into the nighttime made me feel as though I were spying on the secret rooms of Renny Lodge, back in Bridewell. I used to love the way the words would drift up the stairs in the lodge, echoing as I tried to make out their meaning.

"We'll be in Lathbury by morning light. That's very fast indeed."

Both Warvold and his brother, Roland, were smoking pipes. I could see the glow from the embers bright near their faces, the distinct outline of their features against the black of the night. Catherine (who I used to call Renny) was sleeping in the cabin below as Odessa and Balmoral watched over her. Armon the giant and Murphy were somewhere on the deck with me, but I couldn't see where. Lying by myself, I was frightened and wished I could see something more than the shadows of the two men with their pipes. I quietly opened the leather pouch around my neck and removed the last Jocasta. The orange glow was so brilliant it seemed to set the air on fire. I'd never known it to be so bright, so fiery in its intensity, piercing every corner of the darkness. I shielded my eyes and looked around as Armon sat upright, staring into the air as the mist above us was lit by the power of the Jocasta.

"Put it back!" yelled Warvold. "Put it back as quickly as you can!"

I fumbled with the pouch around my neck and dropped the glowing Jocasta inside, then drew up the string. The light vanished as quickly as it had come. Night crept back over the deck of the ship as Warvold and Roland strode quickly over to me and knelt down at my side.

"You must never do that again, Alexa," Warvold warned. "Not at night when we're on the Lonely Sea." He put his hand on my shoulder. "With the covering of clouds this place is unnaturally dark at night. The light of the Jocasta can be seen silhouetted from above the mist in The Land of Elyon."

He looked up then, and even though I could barely make out his face in the light of the glowing embers in his pipe, I could tell he was worried.

"You can be sure there are those who are looking for such a light, not the least of which are the bats — the black swarm — and maybe Victor Grindall himself."

Roland struck a match and lit a small lamp that hung by a ragged old rope at the side of the deck.

"A little light is fine," Roland said. "But that thing you've got there — I've never seen anything like it. If anyone was watching from above, they'd surely have seen the mist aglow in orange."

"Quiet," whispered Warvold.

He put his hand on his pipe and puffed slowly. At first all I could hear was the creaking sound of the old ship on the sea and the wind billowing steadily through the sails. There was something else, though — something far away but coming closer. A strange sound.

"Put out the light," Warvold said to Roland, "and pocket your pipe."

There is a special darkness when you blow out the one lamp in the night, when your eyes still expect light but there is none to be had. It is a total darkness that heightens all the other senses, and on this night I could suddenly hear clearly what Warvold heard.

The sound of a thousand bats shrieking on the wind, their leathery wings beating a mangled drumroll as they came closer.

"Armon!" I screamed. "Where are you? Get belowdecks!" I knew he was the one the bats were after.

I could hear the sound of feet scuffling on the deck, but I couldn't see what was happening around me.

"Hold my hand, Alexa." It was Warvold, whispering near my face. I could smell the sweet tobacco in his beard. We listened to the wind as the sound of the black swarm came nearer still. Warvold guided me along the deck until a door was flung open from the floor and faint light escaped into the night.

"Down you go," said Warvold, holding the door upright while he beckoned me inside. I watched as Murphy scampered between Roland's legs and down the stairs.

"Armon first," I said. "We can't risk having him found."

"He won't fit, Alexa," said Warvold. "He's too big. Now get inside — there's no time to waste."

He prodded me down into the belly of the ship until we were safely below. The door slid down and was locked behind me not a moment too soon.

The black swarm was upon the ship.

The bats were attacking the deck, banging their heads and flapping their wings, clawing everywhere with their tiny black talons. It was a tremendous, horrible noise, and all I could think of was Armon out on the deck, hiding in a corner, trying not to be found. I knew he would put up a valiant fight, but in the end the bats would overtake him and that would be the end of the race of Seraphs, the last of the giants. He would be turned into an ogre, and only ogres would remain.

The clatter on the deck decreased and then stopped altogether, but the bats could still be heard swarming around the ship. Then there was a new sound, a sound of ripping and tearing. Murphy darted across the dimly lit room and landed in my lap, shaking uncontrollably. Balmoral and Odessa instinctively moved to protect Catherine, who had awakened, disoriented and frail.

"They're attacking the sails," said Roland. "It's a good thing the big ones are down. We haven't had need of them with this wind at our back."

The shredding continued for a time, and then the swarm circled the boat again before flying off, the sound of their wings a faint whisper before Warvold spoke.

"It is to our advantage that bats have but a pea for a brain," he said. "They think only of finding Armon, nothing else. Either they've discovered him and have done their terrible work, or they've gone looking elsewhere." Then Warvold fell silent, and we all listened to the creaking of the old ship, the sound of the torn sails flapping in the wind, the last of the bats in the distance.

Murphy jumped from my arms and ran to the top of the steps, scratching on the door in the ceiling to get out. Just then we all heard the same thing, and it stirred a mix of emotions. What we heard was the sound of giant footsteps pounding the deck, walking toward the door. Would it still be Armon, or had the bats found him and transformed him into a beast that would rip the door off its hinges at any moment?

Murphy ran back down the stairs and leaped into my arms. There was a knock at the door in the ceiling, and I yelped at the sound of it.

"Shall I unlock it?" asked Roland.

"I think that would be best," said Warvold. "If he's been turned against us, he'll only knock it in. We don't have much hope if we've got an ogre loose on the ship."

Roland walked up the stairs and pulled away the bolt, then ran back down and stood next to Warvold. Odessa growled, ready to defend us.

The door creaked open, and all we could see was darkness. But one thing was certain — whatever was standing there in the night was dripping something into the room, and my heart skipped with the thought of blood pouring from Armon's broken body.

CHAPTER 2

A VOICE ON THE WIND

The silhouette that looked down at us through the doorway was dark against the night sky. It was huge and unmoving, quiet but for the sound of water falling on the stairs leading down into the cabin of the *Warwick Beacon*.

"They've gone," said Armon. "You can stop your worrying."

He was on his knees, sticking his giant head into the opening so we could see him. His hair was wet, dripping salty water on the stairs, but he was smiling and he was still the giant we all remembered.

I ran up the stairs and put my arms around his big, damp neck. He lifted me up through the doorway as he stood, and I was somewhere high in the night air feeling happy and free, the wind flapping Armon's long wet hair against my face.

"You jumped off the ship?" I said.

"I wasn't going to fit into that doorway," he answered. "So I crept overboard in the darkness and slid into the water, then swam out to sea."

"Why didn't I think of that?" I said.

Concerned the bats might return suddenly, I rejoined the others below. Armon lay down on the deck and poked his head down into the space. Every few seconds he disappeared, swallowed up by the darkness outside, looking and listening for flying intruders. His only companion on the deck was Squire. She'd flown off when the black swarm arrived, but she was back now, flapping here and there on the edges of the ship.

There was a lamp trimmed low sitting between us on the floor. The hour was late, maybe midnight, but everyone was wide awake and listening. The creaking of the old boat on the waves made a constant chatter, but I didn't mind. It was soothing in its own way.

"I'll have to get to those sails sooner than later," said Roland. "We might end up hitting the cliffs if we drift too close in the night."

"The bats are gone," said Armon. "If

they come again I can go back into the water and you can get below."

That was assurance enough for Roland. He took Balmoral, Armon, and a lamp with him to mend the sails. The rest of us sat quietly for a moment listening to them at their work, and in the soft light of the cabin I heard a familiar voice stirring in the air. What it said frightened me, and I sat in the cabin wondering if I should share it with the others.

"Warvold?" I said. He only nodded and looked at me while Odessa and Catherine sat silent.

"Did you know that the last Jocasta makes it so you can hear Elyon's voice?" I looked down at Murphy sitting in my lap, then continued. "Not always, but every now and then. It's the strangest sound, like a whisper on the wind."

"I know of the legend, and I've wondered if it were true," Warvold said. After some hesitation he added, "You must listen carefully for that voice."

I waited a moment more, afraid to say what I thought I'd heard.

"Do you think everything I hear in that voice on the wind is from Elyon, or could it be that Abaddon has found a way to speak to me as well?"

Catherine was still very weak, but she

took my hand then and held it, though she said nothing.

"If it's as the legend said it would be, the voice is that of Elyon alone," Warvold answered. He was sitting next to Catherine, and he brushed a bit of hair away from her face. His mind seemed lost in thought.

"Is there something you want to tell me, something you've heard?" he asked me.

I looked at Catherine, so weak and tired, and I wished she would lie down and go back to sleep.

"Yes," I said. "I've heard something just now that I'm afraid to tell."

Before I could explain further, Roland came barreling down the stairs with Balmoral close behind.

"I've taken down the torn sails and raised the larger one," Roland said. "I know these waters well and can guide us in the darkness. We should be approaching Lathbury just as the sun comes up."

"That's good, Roland — but wait a moment," Warvold replied. "Alexa, have you got something to say to us?"

"I do," I answered; then I squeezed Catherine's hand a little tighter and told them what I'd heard on the wind:

"The voice I heard said we couldn't all stay in Lathbury."

"Why not?" Odessa asked. It was the first thing she'd said in quite a while. Because of the Jocasta, I was the only human who could understand her.

"We can leave Catherine there," I said, "but the rest of us must go on."

Warvold contemplated this bit of news as he relit his pipe, the sight of which seemed to interest Roland and Balmoral. They both sat down on the steps leading down into the cabin and pulled out their own pipes, preparing them as Warvold sat thinking.

I knew from talking with Warvold that there would be a rope waiting for us at Lathbury, running down the length of the cliffs and almost into the water. It had hung there a long time, but Warvold wouldn't tell us who had put it there. As far as we knew, this was our only escape from the Lonely Sea — at least according to Warvold.

"There's more," I said.

"I thought as much," said Warvold. He fiddled with his pipe and blew smoke over his head.

Murphy sat nearby, his tail twitching wildly. He spoke quickly and with purpose.

"Does the voice on the wind say anything about finding nuts or treats hidden away on this old boat?"

I smiled and patted him once on the head before continuing.

"We only have five days to bring Grindall the stone or we'll never see Yipes alive again. We must rescue Yipes, and I thought we would leave Catherine in Lathbury and go directly to Bridewell to find him. But it seems that right now we are meant to go somewhere else. There's something Elyon wants us to see, something beyond Turlock, at the point of land farthest away from the Dark Tower."

Roland stopped puffing at his pipe and sat dumbstruck by the news. For an instant he seemed unsure what to say. He was either terribly excited or dreadfully scared — I couldn't tell which by the look on his face.

"Alexa, are you sure about what you heard? Could you have heard it wrong?" he asked me.

I told him I was sure. I knew what I'd heard. It was unmistakable.

"There's something you should know then," he said. He put his pipe back into the corner of his mouth and puffed three quick times. "I have sailed the Lonely Sea for many years, exploring faraway places with secrets and mysteries hard to imagine.

But there is one place I have never gone. The place you speak of, beyond Turlock on the far side of The Land of Elyon, is utterly impassable with this ship."

He looked down into the room from the step where he sat and thought a moment before speaking again.

"Fierce winds never die there — they just push everything into the cliffs. No sooner would we round the corner of Turlock and the *Warwick Beacon* would be smashed to bits against the rocks."

Roland kept on, explaining that the place I spoke of was so dangerous he'd never even considered going there. Only once had he tried to approach it, from miles offshore. The winds had been so strong that they nearly capsized the boat before he veered off and ended up all the way near Ainsworth.

"Still," Roland finished, "it would be quite an adventure to try." A smile crept over his face, and his eyes went glassy and distant.

Warvold looked at Catherine, her eyes barely open and her skin a pale white chalk.

"Are you *sure,* Alexa?" he asked.

I nodded, convinced of what I'd heard. I could tell he was troubled by the idea of leaving Catherine's side again.

"We'll need to get Catherine off the boat where she can regain her strength," he decided. "This journey will be too much for her."

He looked at his brother and asked him a question. "Can you stop us at Lathbury, as we'd planned, before we go racing around the corner into the cliffs?"

"I can," Roland answered, and he went along merrily puffing his pipe, the adventurer in him already thinking of the untold dangers that awaited us.

We all sat silent then, wondering what to do. I was worried for Yipes, but I was also scared to go around the corner from Turlock. It seemed that the Lonely Sea was angry in those parts . . . and I didn't see how we could overcome the jagged cliffs that awaited us.

CHAPTER 3

THE STORM

As the sun rose I could see light creeping into the mist above. It made me feel much better as we all milled around the deck waiting for Roland to tell us where we were. Warvold had been particularly quiet all morning, preparing to leave Catherine behind yet again.

As we arrived at the base of Lathbury, Roland pulled the ship closer to the cliffs, but not so close that we were in danger of crashing against the rocks. Roland had a small, two-person boat on deck that he held over the sea on ropes and poles. When the small boat was clear of the *Warwick Beacon*, he let out the ropes until the little vessel bobbed softly on the water. The seas were calm, an ominous silence before the storms that awaited us beyond Turlock.

Warvold sat alone with Catherine, and they whispered to each other things I couldn't hear. I couldn't take my eyes off them, and I was surprised to see them looking my way more than once as they spoke. There was something special about these two, a connection I felt to them that I couldn't quite understand. Seeing them huddled together made me feel sad that they were parting again so soon.

Eventually, the two of them walked slowly over to the rest of us. Catherine gave me a hug, squeezing my little bones tightly in her grasp.

"You be careful now," she said. Then she released me and looked deep into my eyes. "I'll be waiting for you in Lathbury."

I was excited to get back home, to see not only her but my father and mother as well. It had been a long journey, but as I watched Catherine carefully climb down to the small boat I felt certain the most dangerous stretch remained. I wondered if I would ever see her again.

Warvold got into the boat with her and paddled them the short distance to the cliffs where we could all see a red flag hanging from a rope against the rocks. This rope was very thick and even had a seat of leather hanging at its bottom. Who-ever put it there was expecting to haul people up the sheer cliffs. I was terribly curious who it might be.

Warvold got Catherine settled in the seat, kissed her, then pulled hard on the rope three times. There was a long pause, and then we all watched as the rope lurched to life and Catherine was carried up the side of the cliff, far into the air, until she disappeared into the mist. When I looked back to Warvold, he was already halfway back to our boat. Squire landed on the front of the little dinghy, keeping him company on the Lonely Sea.

"That can't have been easy," said Murphy, sitting on my shoulder. "It makes me wonder about Yipes, all alone with those awful ogres. I hope he'll be all right."

I felt awful that we couldn't all go up the rope together and make plans to sneak into Bridewell and rescue him. I was mystified that Elyon was sending us by another way, into a place Roland didn't even think we could survive.

Once Warvold was back on board, Roland lifted the undamaged sails, and the early morning flew by quickly. We approached, then passed around Turlock, the winds not quite as strong as Roland had remembered them.

"Could it be that the winds have finally tired of their constant blowing?" he said.

No sooner had the words left his mouth than the winds became more violent, the waves crashing against the ship and pushing it toward the cliffs. Rain came tumbling out of the sky like no rain I'd ever seen before. It felt as though the sky above us had waited for our arrival and held on to more and more water, month after month, only to drop it all on the *Warwick Beacon*.

There was a sound then, a roaring from the east, and we all turned to see what it was. Through the driving rain we all saw the wind coming straight at us. We could see it off in the distance lifting the water into great waves. The storm didn't creep up on our boat like a cat will sneak up on a mouse. It leaped on top of us all at once without warning, and we began to tumble on the waves toward the cliffs.

We were barely around the corner of Turlock, and already something was set against us. There was no place for us here, only the rocks and the bottom of the sea. We had ventured into a place we should not have.

"We must turn back!" shouted Roland. "There's still time to swing her around and escape the storm!"

Just then a giant wave rolled over the

ship, and we were all left scrambling for a hold. When I could see again, I saw Warvold advancing on me quickly.

"Get below with Murphy and Odessa!" he yelled. "We'll turn her around and try to get out."

I did as I was told and began scrambling across the deck as quickly as I could, holding on to the rail as I went. I looked out into the raging sea just in time to see another wave about to hit the boat, this one bigger than all the rest. I held on as tightly as I could, but it was no use. I flew free with the wave, out into the Lonely Sea.

It was strangely quiet under the water, like holding a pillow over my ears when there were storms back home. It was almost serene compared to the storm raging overhead. The sound of the rain pelting the sea made me feel as if I was under a giant blanket, a thousand tiny pebbles bouncing off the surface.

Don't let them turn back.

In the quiet of the water I heard these five words and I didn't understand them. How could Elyon want for us to be smashed against the rocks or capsized on the Lonely Sea? I felt a blow on my back, and I thought I'd landed in the rocks.

To my surprise I was lifted out of the water, into the wrath of the storm, then set down on the deck of the *Warwick Beacon*.

"Are you all right?" Armon yelled, trying to overcome the sound of the howling wind. He had plucked me out of the sea with his giant hands.

"I'm okay!" I shouted back, wiping the water from my eyes and face. "Where's everyone else?"

Armon pointed to the front of the boat where the three men — Warvold, Balmoral, and Roland — were trying to turn the wheel and face the ship back toward Turlock.

I ran across the slippery deck as more waves crashed over the boat.

"Don't do that! Keep going into the storm!" I screamed.

"Have you gone mad?" yelled Roland. "We can't make it, Alexa. If we don't turn back now we'll be thrown into the rocks."

Warvold crawled across the deck on his hands and knees until he met with me, rain running down his face. He took hold of both my shoulders.

"Are you sure, Alexa?"

I looked at him pleadingly and nodded, though I couldn't have expected him to trust me.

"Stay the course!" yelled Warvold. "Point her straight down the side of the cliffs and hang on!"

Roland and Balmoral looked stunned, and I wondered if they might throw us belowdecks and turn back anyway. Armon came alongside the men and put to rest any such thoughts they might have had. He took the wheel in his mighty hands and turned it a few times around, heading us perfectly parallel to the cliffs and away from Turlock.

I crawled over to the wheel, and Armon put one of his hands around my waist and lifted me to his side, determined not to let me tumble overboard again. And then we all held on and prayed that the waves wouldn't push us into the cliffs and bring our adventure to an end.

We were a hundred feet from the rocks and closing the gap fast. A short time more and the *Warwick Beacon* would be dashed against the cliffs. I began to think of all the things we'd accomplished, only to find ourselves caught in a storm we couldn't escape. We were utterly helpless against its fury. I looked up at Armon, and he smiled at me, the beads of water running around his eyes and his big nose, and I remembered how I'd felt this very same way when we were pinned down in the Dark Hills, the ogres walking out to find us. Armon had appeared as if out of the very air, and we were saved. Unlikely as it seemed, I had to believe Elyon had some plan we couldn't understand that would protect the *Warwick Beacon* from the cliffs.

The storm seemed to reach its peak, waves and wind rushing in from all sides, the boat tossed on the Lonely Sea like a feather twisting in a gale. We were spinning around in circles, and I was losing any sense of where we were.

"Something's not right about this!" It was Roland, yelling into the storm. He was frantically turning his head from side to side trying to figure out where the cliffs were in all the rain as the ship continued to spin uncontrollably.

"The storm has changed, and for once I'm excited to say that it's gotten much worse!"

The Lonely Sea must have finally sent poor Roland into a fit of hysteria. He was laughing uncontrollably, throwing back his head as he held the rail of his beloved ship.

"He's gone mad!" said Balmoral.

"No, he hasn't," said Warvold. "He's right. The winds are coming down the cliffs directly at us just as the winds from the sea are pushing us into them. We're at the center of the storm, where two forces push against each other."

We all looked on in awe as the *Warwick Beacon* stopped spinning and righted its course parallel with the cliffs only a hundred feet away. Warvold was right. Wind was billowing both down from the cliffs and in from the Lonely Sea, two forces set against each other, our ship now stuck in the middle of the two.

The storm did not subside. If anything it grew fiercer as the two sides pushed against each other equally, shooting us down the middle of the eye of the storm.

"Everyone belowdecks!" yelled Roland. And then he looked at Armon. "Everyone but you."

It was the only thing to do. If we stayed out in the storm much longer, one of us was sure to go overboard. Armon set me down on the slippery deck. I huddled together with Balmoral and Warvold, and we slowly made our way back to the door in the floor that led to the cabin. Balmoral flung it open, and it was nearly torn free in the storm as water rushed down into the belly of the ship. Warvold pushed me inside, and I turned one last time. Through the driving rain I saw Armon standing over

Roland, the two of them holding the wheel steady. Roland wasn't about to miss the storm of his life.

I stumbled down the stairs, followed by Warvold. Then Balmoral heaved the door shut behind him with a mighty bang, and we were sealed in with Odessa and Murphy.

The *Warwick Beacon* rolled back and forth on the sea, creaking with every crashing wave, and I thought the whole ship would be blown apart. I wondered where Squire had gone off to, if she'd cleared the clouds and was watching the storm from above.

Hours passed as we waited in the damp hull of the ship, hanging on to beams as we rocked back and forth on the waves. I kept thinking the storm would shift and we would crash into the cliffs at any moment. I wondered if our friends were even on the deck any longer, or if they'd been thrown clear into the raging sea.

It was a terrible, long day that seemed to go on forever.

CHAPTER 4

THE CLIFFS

“There are nine cities that I know of in The Land of Elyon.” It was Warvold, speaking the words over the sound of the storm outside. It was hard to tell how long we’d been belowdecks, but it was a long time indeed.

I had found a corner to sit in where I wouldn’t be thrown from side to side as the boat rocked violently. Murphy sat in my lap, as was his habit. Either he was more frightened than usual — or he was cold, because he wouldn’t stop shivering.

“Nine cities that I’ve seen with my own eyes,” Warvold continued, and then he proceeded to whisper each of them too quietly for me to hear, though I knew their names.

Bridewell, Turlock, Lathbury, Lunenburg, Ainsworth, the Western Kingdom, Castalia, and the two Northern Kingdoms.

“But there is one other,” Warvold said

aloud. "One I thought could never be reached."

He sat silent and steadied himself at the sound of another wave hitting the ship.

"The Tenth City," he told us. "Beyond the Sly Field and through the eternal mist, in a place no one has ever found. I wonder if we might see this place before too long, if this old boat can find its way."

There was very little light to be had belowdecks, only what was cast inside from the cracks where drops of water came in. But I could see the twinkling in Warvold's eyes, as if he'd spoken of a treasure he'd long thought unattainable, now suddenly within reach.

"I wouldn't get your hopes up too high," said Odessa. "Even the animals have searched for such a place, but none have found it. It may be that it's only in our imagination, put there to remind us of who created all this."

I told Warvold what the wolf had said, and we were all met with a long silence from our old friend.

"You may be right, Odessa," he finally answered. "But something tells me if it's a real place, I'm closer to it now than I've ever been. I've traveled the whole of The Land of Elyon and turned over most of the rocks on my way. But the mist beyond the Sly Field is impassable. Somehow it doesn't matter where you go in. The Sly Field always spits you back out again, farther away from where you were trying to go."

I piped in then, interested in what Warvold was saying.

"I read a book once about a man named Cabeza de Vaca. He tried to find the Tenth City, but he got lost, just like you. He finally gave up trying."

"I knew him well," Warvold replied, a slight smile on his face. "Cabeza and I compared notes, but nothing came of it. It's as if whatever lies beyond the field of mist is hidden for some purpose we can't understand. Either that or some riddle keeps us from it."

The sea seemed to calm for a moment, and we rolled up and down on a large, slow wave. Warvold broke the silence as though he hadn't even noticed the storm had turned less violent.

"The Tenth City," he said. "The most secret place, a place untouched by human or beast — and we may yet stumble onto it if we can overcome the storm."

Just as he said it, the door to the cabin flew open, and Roland came bounding down the stairs two at a time. The light from outside was faint, and I understood immediately that we'd passed through the entire day and were approaching late afternoon. A few more hours and night would return.

Roland, dripping wet and breathless, held on to the beam next to the stairs and yelled at us all.

"The storm still rages on, but it's come down a notch. It's the strangest thing. We've been pushed closer to the cliffs, but that unexplainable wind coming off the rock face keeps holding us away from crashing into the rocks. The storm from the sea seems to have worn itself out, and it, too, is less fierce."

"It sounds as though the rains have stopped as well," said Balmoral.

"They have," answered Roland. "Might you take the wheel for a spell if I show you how it's done?"

Balmoral was up on his feet immediately and walking for the door.

"Anything would be better than sitting down here any longer," he complained. He was up the stairs and out the door before Roland could change his mind. Warvold and Odessa followed, then Roland disappeared back into what remained of the storm on deck.

For some reason I stayed where I was. Something about what I would see when I went outside scared me.

"Murphy?" I said.

"Yes?"

"Will you promise to stay with me no matter what?"

He leaped out of my hands onto my shoulder, digging his little claws into my wet clothing.

"I promise," he said.

"All right, then. Stay where you are and hold on tight. I have word from Elyon, and I can't do what I'm told without you. I'm too frightened."

Murphy swung his head around and tried to catch my eye. We looked at each other in the dimly lit cabin, and he smiled and chirped.

"I just love being in on all the secret things, don't you?"

I only nodded and patted him on the head. Then I got up, marched over to the stairs, and climbed up into the light of day.

The storm had settled, but winds still billowed on both sides of the boat, holding it steady about a hundred feet off the cliffs. Everyone was gathered around the captain's wheel where Balmoral was keeping the *Warwick Beacon* steadily parallel to the cliffs. I caught Armon's eye and motioned for him to come see me, and he broke away from the group.

He bent down on one knee and lowered his giant head down toward me.

"Armon, there's something you must help me with, but I'm not sure you're going to want to do it," I said.

Armon turned back to look at the group of men standing together with Odessa, then we both looked up and watched as Squire shot through the mist and held steady in the driving wind. A moment later she turned once over the boat and flew back into the mist to places we couldn't see. I wondered then if the storm was happening above the mist as well, or if it was contained below on the Lonely Sea. It was an odd thought to imagine a pristine day above while a storm raged below, but it seemed to me that this might be the way of things. Elyon and Abaddon were fighting each other, the strength of both focused entirely on the *Warwick Beacon* and the treasure it held. It wasn't so hard to believe that things back home might have remained quite ordinary.

Armon turned back to me as if he knew what I was about to ask of him.

"What would you like me to do?" he asked.

Just then Squire shot out of the mist once more between the *Warwick Beacon* and the cliffs, where she hung in the air over the Lonely Sea.

"Can you swim in these waters? Can you make it to the cliffs with me riding on your back?"

"And me!" squeaked Murphy.

Armon stood up and seemed to size up the task.

"I take it only the three of us can go?" he said.

I looked down at the little bag holding the Jocasta and nodded. Without another word spoken, Armon looked once more at the group by the wheel. The only one looking our way with some interest was Odessa. The rest were talking among themselves. Armon picked me up and threw me over his back. Murphy held tightly to my clothing with his claws, and I wrapped my arms around Armon's neck. Then the giant leaped into the air so high and so far it was as though we were flying. I looked back and saw Warvold staring at us in wonder, alarmed at this new development.

We hit the water, Armon taking the full blow, and then he was swimming fast for the cliffs. I held on and felt the salty chill of the sea. Murphy was digging in a little too much and caught hold of my skin.

"Murphy, not so tight!"

"So sorry — it's all so exciting, isn't it?" He let go his grip enough for my skin to escape his little claws.

Squire flew out of the mist ahead and down over us, screeching loudly. Then she circled low over our heads and darted for the cliffs. She landed, and I knew for sure what we were supposed to do.

"Elyon said to follow Squire — that she would lead us where we need to go."

Armon seemed to understand and changed his course slightly. I looked back over my shoulder and saw that Roland was trying to turn the boat and come after us. I waved him off, but it was no use — he kept fighting the storm, trying to right the ship in ways that forces around him would not allow. The winds came up once more, and the storm billowed heavier, pushing the ship out to sea even as Armon pulled us over the last of the big waves toward the cliffs.

Squire was sitting on the rocks screeching over and over as we approached. Armon gave one last stroke, then braced himself as a wave threw us onto the rocks. He held on to the jagged stone, wind roaring down the face of the cliff. Squire was just to our left, and she kept up her screeching until Armon side-stepped over to her and we discovered for the first time that she sat in front of a rather large, dark opening in the rocks. Armon quickly jumped inside the space as Squire flew away. Armon's back was heaving up and down as he tried to catch his breath. The cave we'd found protected us from the wind and allowed us to rest a moment.

"The Lonely Sea just about took all the strength of a giant," said Murphy. His matted, wet fur made him look scrawny, like a soaked kitten.

"That it did," grunted Armon. He was regaining his strength, but the swim had been more of a challenge than even I'd thought it would be. It had tested the giant's strength, and he'd almost come up short, which worried me as I looked out to the sea. Would he have the strength it would take to get us back to the *Warwick Beacon*?

Squire re-emerged, flying straight at us. I had an uneasy feeling about where she would be flying next. My worries were confirmed when she turned sharply upward the moment she reached us. We peeked our heads out into the storm and watched as she labored against the wind all the way up the side of the cliffs and into the mist, where we could see her no more.

Armon looked over his shoulder at us and found Murphy and me hoping for some reassurance that he could scale the cliffs. He sighed mightily and looked at his own hands in the weak light of the crevice — we all looked at them. I leaned over and put my hand against his, then Murphy ran down my arm and put his paw on the back of my hand — my hand so much bigger than Murphy's paw, Armon's hand that much bigger still than mine.

"If I had hands that big *I* could do it," said Murphy, and for some reason Armon thought this was very funny, and he began to laugh. He stretched out his arms and his back rumbled and cracked against my chest.

"Off we go then," he said. "Before the light starts to fade."

Armon crept out into the wind and took hold of the side of the cliff. Then he began climbing, the two friends on his back shivering with fright at each new step.

CHAPTER 5

TELL NO ONE WHAT YOU'VE SEEN

We were high on the cliff — almost into the mist — when I looked down for the first time. That was a mistake.

Armon had lost his footing and his big leg swung free in the wet air. Looking down made me gasp, but I couldn't stop looking. We were far above the ground, and I could see the waters crashing along the rocks below. I also saw the *Warwick Beacon*, and I hoped Warvold and the others could see us. They had drifted farther out to sea, and I suddenly felt we'd made a terrible mistake. Our companions must have thought we'd lost our minds, but there was nothing they could do to help us or stop us, and it looked as though we might not be able to get back to the boat as it drifted away. A lump caught in my throat, and I began to feel dizzy. I buried my head into Armon's back and promised myself not to look down again.

As Armon lumbered farther up the cliff, struggling for every footing and gasping for air as he went, I tried to take my mind off the fact that the three of us would fall to our deaths if Armon lost his grip on the slippery rock face. I imagined that Warvold and Roland were standing on the boat feeling a little jealous, which actually made quite a bit of sense. The two of them would have wished it were them on the back of a giant, scaling a seemingly unassailable cliff to places no one had ever seen. It put a smile on my face to think that in some ways I'd become their equal, ways I would not have dreamed possible growing up in Lathbury. And then I opened my eyes again and looked up.

The air was thick and moist. We had entered the mist — which meant, I hoped, we were nearing the top of the cliff. We weren't able to see more than a few feet in any direction — an alarming development, since Armon was having enough trouble finding the few places where he could hold on. Now they were even fewer to choose from. But there was one wonderful thing that happened when we entered the clouds that I couldn't quite understand.

The storm was gone.

The higher we rose in the mist, the less wind and rain there was. We could hear the storm below us, but it was strangely peaceful now, as though we had entered another realm entirely. I watched as Armon's arms extended beyond where I could see, his hands crawling from place to place along the cliff, looking for a hold above.

"I'm scared, Armon," I said. "What if we can't get back down?"

He didn't answer me, and it seemed he'd sensed something above that gave him a new strength that only made him move higher and higher at a startling pace. Time passed quickly, and light began to pierce our world of mist. And then, without warning, we were out in a perfectly cloudless afternoon, another fifty feet of cliff above us that was dry to the touch and full of good holds in every direction.

"I have a feeling about this place I can't explain," Armon told me. "Something I haven't felt in a very long time."

Murphy chimed in: "The only feeling I have is that a squirrel shouldn't be climbing so high. This altitude makes my fur feel funny." He held on with three paws and used the fourth to scratch behind his ear like a dog.

Armon wasn't breathing so hard now, and he seemed all the more superhuman to me as he practically leaped from hold to hold on the rock face, taking us higher and higher until we were all the way to the top, and he crawled over the edge and onto The Land of Elyon.

"Stay on my back," he said. He crawled on his hands and knees away from the edge, and I wondered if he was afraid a gust of wind might blow us into the air and down to the jagged rocks below. When he was well clear of the edge, Armon stood up. I looked over his shoulder at the place we'd arrived.

What we saw was both magnificent and frightening in ways I had never experienced before. I had hoped we were being led to a city or a mountain, but what I saw wasn't that at all. Murphy darted back and forth between Armon's shoulders, trying to see everything in front of him. I only stared in disbelief, my breathing choppy as though the very air around me had gone thin and hard to find.

Armon was walking ever so slowly forward, as though a force beyond his control was drawing him. No one spoke, not even

Murphy, and then out of the air came a crystal voice with words I hadn't imagined I'd hear — words I didn't want to hear.

Tell no one what you've seen.

The voice was clearer than before, not on the wind as it had been in the past. I almost expected Armon and Murphy to hear, too — but they didn't. I hoped there would be more for me to tell them, but there was nothing.

Armon continued to walk closer to what lay before us, and then a brutal wind came up and nearly knocked him off his feet. A great cloud of white rushed over the land and began covering everything in front of us. A few minutes later, as we braced against the wind at the edge of the cliffs, what we'd seen was gone.

"Armon, you can't tell anyone about this place," I said. "You, too, Murphy. No one can know."

Neither of them spoke, and it seemed to me that we all understood Elyon had brought us to this very place for his own purpose.

He said something else to me then. Something that, if I followed, would be the start of a plan. I was afraid to share it with anyone when I heard it, but I knew I would have to tell Armon later. I had to think about it first. I had to figure out the exact meaning of Elyon's words.

"We have to go," said Armon. "If I don't leave now, I won't be able to."

Armon turned away from the land before us and craned his neck to look at me where I rested my head on his shoulder. It was clear from the glimmer in his eyes that turning back was very difficult for him. He swung his whole body around and looked out over the mist that covered the Lonely Sea.

"I only hope we can make it back to the *Warwick Beacon*," he said. Then we were over the side heading down, visions of what we'd seen lodged in all our heads as we went.

The descent was much faster than the way up, as Armon moved like a giant spider along the sheer cliff wall, down through the mist, back into the storm below, and finally stood among the rocks at the base. Armon only rested for a few seconds before stepping into the Lonely Sea and swimming for the boat. It was a long way off, but we could see it in the distance, bobbing on the waves. The storm seemed to push us out to sea, so Armon had only to guide us in the right direction. The light of day was almost gone as we approached the *Warwick Beacon*, Warvold and Roland and Balmoral yelling our names and waving us in. In the weakening light, a rope was thrown into the sea, and Armon took hold of it.

When Armon finally climbed over the edge of the *Warwick Beacon*, he set down Murphy and me and collapsed on the deck, his huge body sprawled out before us, chest heaving as rain pelted his face.

Murphy was so pitiful-looking with his wet, matted fur. All his bones were showing through and his little face looked exhausted, as though he might fall away sleeping and roll down the deck of the ship.

"Wait till I get back home and tell everyone I went swimming in the ocean and climbed to the top of the cliffs," he said. "They'll never believe me."

Warvold picked me up and hugged me so hard I thought I would burst.

"Please don't ever do anything like that again," he whispered in my ear. Then he turned to his brother and yelled, "Get us out of here! We're nearly around the edge of the cliffs."

He carried me belowdecks and threw a soggy blanket around me.

"Are you all right? Are you hurt? What

did you see? What's up there, Alexa?" He was overcome with curiosity and concern, and it nearly broke my heart to sit there shaking my head, unable to tell him what I longed to share.

I sat shivering with Warvold's arms around me as the *Warwick Beacon* carried me away from a place I would never forget and could not understand — a secret place I could tell no one about.

CHAPTER 6

SEPARATED

I remember getting sleepy. I was wet and miserable and dreaming I was in the smoking room at Renny Lodge, curled up on a velvety couch with a good book and a cup of tea, a big fire burning, pipe smoke swirling around the room. And then I don't remember much of anything until I awoke with light peeking through the door that led up the stairs to the deck of the *Warwick Beacon*.

I sat up, awake at the sight of it, thinking the storm would blow in and rouse everyone. Then I realized I was no longer cold and the storm no longer raged outside. There was a warm light pouring down the stairs and a soft morning breeze fluttering around the room. Someone had picked me up in the night and set me in a hammock, where I was warm but still a little moist. I jumped down from the hammock, awake and running for the stairs, excited to see a peaceful day unfolding.

The air outside was right between cool and warm, the crispness of the morning passed but the heat of the day yet to stir. The Lonely Sea was calm but for a few waves drifting lazily on the surface. I looked to my left and saw the cliffs rising into the mist a hundred yards off.

"Ahhh, you've finally woken up." Warvold's kindly voice came from the wheel where he stood with Roland, wind dancing in their hair, ideas of adventure evident on their faces. The two of them had known only risk and danger all their lives, and the reward was the look I saw in their eyes. They were two people full of life to the point of bursting, and I wanted only to be more like them.

"You look as though you've seen a ghost," said Roland as he turned the wheel ever so slightly toward the cliffs.

"She looks well," said Warvold. "Much better than she ought to after the perils of only a day ago."

He walked over to me, and we strode hand in hand to the very front of the *Warwick Beacon*, where we stood looking out into the sea. I turned back to see Armon and Balmoral mending the sails,

Murphy sitting on Odessa's back as the great wolf slept at their feet.

"Alexa," said Warvold. "We're nearing Ainsworth, where things will get more complicated. Will you stay with me a moment and let me tell you a few things?"

I was glad to hear we were close to a place where we might regain our footing on land and go after Yipes. We were already starting our third day's journey from Castalia. Only two days remained before Grindall expected me in Bridewell with the last stone.

"Will we be able to reach land, to rescue Yipes?" I asked Warvold.

"That we will. There are a few more surprises I have yet to reveal." He stared out to sea and smiled serenely. "My years in Bridewell may have been lacking in adventure, but they were an important season. I contemplated many things behind the shadows of the walls. I laid many plans." He turned away from the Lonely Sea and looked at me. "Before that — during all those years of my youth, wandering in The Land of Elyon — do you know why I searched, Alexa?" he asked me. It was a question he strained to produce, and he seemed desperate to tell me the answer.

"Because you love adventure, you and

Roland both," I answered.

He looked back out to the sea once more, and his voice trembled as he spoke the true answer.

"I was seized by the power of a great affection."

It seemed as though Warvold had given me the key to his entire life in that one statement, and yet I struggled to understand what he meant. I rolled the words over in my head, trying to see in them what had driven him to live such a dangerous life. *I was seized by the power of a great affection.*

"I don't understand what you mean," I admitted.

Warvold looked deep into my eyes, the wind blowing strands of white and gray hair across his worn face.

"Elyon has only one hope for us, Alexa. That we would know he loves us. Do you understand? The one who made you, the one who made everything." He swept his hand across the sea. "He loves you. And more than that, there is nothing you or I need do to earn his reckless affection for us. That love has driven me to fight his enemy, the enemy of us all."

"Abaddon," I whispered.

He stared at me then with such intensity

I could hardly hold his gaze.

"No evil can resist the power of love forever." He winked at me and smiled, as if he thought that somehow our band of misfits might yet overcome Grindall and the ogres — even Abaddon himself.

"I have failed, and failed, and failed again," he said. "But no amount of failure can move Elyon's hand of affection away from me. It's inescapable. To live boldly for that kind of love is the least I can do."

I suddenly felt that I, too, was seized by this power of great affection, and I understood why I longed to search and search for adventure. What I'd seen with Armon and Murphy at the edge of the cliffs only gave me more strength to carry on.

"We're nearing the cliffs," he said.

I was surprised to look over and see that we were indeed much closer to the rocks. Everyone on deck seemed to be preparing in one way or another for our departure from the *Warwick Beacon*.

"Find your bag, Alexa. We're soon to leave the Lonely Sea."

I gathered my things quickly and joined Armon near the back of the ship, where he stood with Odessa, Murphy, and Balmoral. Everyone but Armon seemed nervous as they looked at the face of the cliffs, wondering what dangers awaited us as the day unfolded.

"There, to the right," said Balmoral. I strained to see where he was pointing and saw the red flag dangling at the bottom of the rope. Warvold crept up behind us and put his hand on my shoulder.

"Our escape from the sea," he said. "I must say I surprise even myself sometimes."

Roland moved the *Warwick Beacon* closer to the rocks and then told us we'd have to swim the rest of the way.

"She's taken quite a beating already. I'm afraid even a scratch on the bottom might break her to pieces."

Roland was very caring toward the *Warwick Beacon*. It sometimes seemed as though the two of them were married to each other, facing the Lonely Sea together as the days slipped into years.

I took a last bite from the breakfast Roland had given us — dried fish and a crust of bread — and then I asked Warvold who was to go first.

"Why, you, of course," he answered. "Armon can carry you along with the animals. We've already discussed it. He feels quite certain that the rope won't be necessary, though I've warned him he'd better at least tie it around his waist in case he loses his footing."

Armon looked down at us and nodded his approval with a smile. He had a strange contraption made of old sails on his back, and I realized it was there to hold me, Murphy, and Odessa as he climbed. He bent down low, and Balmoral helped Warvold set Odessa inside the cloth container. She howled and fidgeted, then lay still on one side of Armon's enormous back. I crawled in on the other side and sat down, my legs hanging free in the air. Murphy had it the easiest — he simply jumped onto my lap and scampered along until he sat on Armon's shoulder and dug his claws in for the journey.

"This isn't as exciting as it was the first time," said Murphy. "Without the storm and the uncertainty of Armon's skill, it's almost boring."

Armon smiled and stood up, lifting us high in the air. Then he started over the edge of the boat once more and slipped into the water up to his waist.

"Hang on, everybody," he said. "Off we go."

He began swimming. Odessa whimpered and thrashed as the water came up to our necks.

"Alexa!" cried Warvold. "There's one thing more I need to tell you. It's very important. I'll tell you as soon as we all reach land."

"All right!" I yelled back. It seemed I would never exhaust all the secrets Warvold held.

Before long we were at the cliffs. Armon wrapped the rope around his waist and pulled on it three times. The rope tightened but Armon didn't move. He seemed to be enjoying himself.

"Whoever's up there is probably wondering whether or not they've caught a whale," he said, putting one massive hand around the rope. "If I give it a good pull, do you think they'll come tumbling over the edge?"

We all begged him not to do it, though we knew he was only playing and would never do such a thing.

As he began to climb I had a whirlwind of thoughts running through my head. Could we save Yipes? Who was holding the rope above the mist? When would Elyon speak to me again?

I rolled these thoughts over in my head until we were only a few feet from the mist, and everything started feeling cool and moist. Armon seemed to have mastered climbing the cliffs, moving with great speed and efficiency. The ride was almost serene.

Then something frightening happened. The wind began to blow from the side. At first it was just a steady breeze, but only a few seconds more and it was gusting. Armon held tightly to the wall. The gusts blew harder and harder.

I yelled at Armon, "Why are you waiting? The wind will die off in the mist if you go only a few more steps."

There was a brief silence, followed by a question I hadn't thought of.

"Where's the *Warwick Beacon*, Alexa? I can't turn around to see it."

I swung my head out of the pouch and looked down, hoping to see the boat close by. To my horror it had already moved an alarming distance down the side of the cliff, and it was being pushed farther away with every second. I could barely see Roland and Balmoral fighting with the wheel, trying to right the sails. The wind was ferocious on the water. Warvold stood at the edge of the boat and looked in my direction, hopelessly being carried away on the wind.

"We have to go back, Armon!" I yelled. "They're being blown away!"

Murphy had scampered down my back and lay in my lap out of the wind. Odessa howled as I held Murphy's shivering little body and watched as the *Warwick Beacon* drifted quickly out of sight.

"I can't get down in this driving wind, Alexa." It was Armon, his voice full of distress. "It's getting worse. We'll have to get into the mist if we're going to survive."

Let them go.

It was the voice on the wind saying words I couldn't imagine following. I *needed* Warvold. Without him I was lost.

Armon began climbing cautiously again, taking each footing and handhold with great care. As his first hand disappeared into the mist, a monstrous gust blew in and knocked his feet clear of the cliff.

He lost his grip with one hand, and suddenly we were dangling over the rocks below.

CHAPTER 7

WHAT HAPPENED WHILE WE WERE AWAY

As we swung back and forth in the wind, I looked out into the open water below and found that the *Warwick Beacon* had drifted so far away it was only a speck in the distance. At least Warvold and the rest were spared from having to see us in such peril.

Murphy jumped out of my lap and ran up to Armon's shoulder, digging in deeply with his claws as he went. When he reached his favorite spot he leaned over and, to my astonishment, bit Armon right on the ear.

Armon thrashed his head and screamed, pulling Murphy into the air. But the little squirrel wouldn't let go of Armon's ear. He looked like a large furry earring dangling in the wind.

Armon seemed to come alive though, the

pain bringing forth some new rush of energy. He righted his feet under himself, grabbed hold of the cliff with his dangling hand, and quick like a lizard crawled up the rock face. The winds were calm the moment we entered the mist, and things felt under control again.

"Sorry about that," said Murphy. I could see well enough in the mist to find that Armon had taken Murphy by the middle and was holding him out in the air, staring at him. Blood was dripping off the giant's ear, but not as much as I would have thought. Armon's skin was leather thick, and Murphy had only barely broken the surface with his sharp teeth.

"You can set me down now, if you would," said Murphy, his squeaky voice cracking and scared. Armon held him there a little longer.

"That hurt," the giant said. "But it probably saved us."

Armon set Murphy down on his shoulder and turned back to his work at the cliffs.

I was overcome with fear as we went through the mist and into the light of a bright blue day. We were separated from Warvold again, and I felt we'd lost our guide. Then, about twenty feet from the top, I heard a familiar voice that made me feel quite a lot better.

"What in the world is *that* thing?" the voice asked. I looked up and saw Nicolas, Warvold's son, peeking his head over the edge of the cliff. Then another head popped out — to stare down in astonishment. Pervis Kotcher's.

"It's a giant," Pervis said.

"No wonder the rope was so heavy!" said Nicolas. "Is it friendly?"

"Ask him yourself," Pervis offered. I could see from where we hung below that he was fooling with Nicolas. Pervis knew something about giants.

Nicolas leaned out over the cliff and watched as we came closer still, only ten feet from the edge.

"Friend or foe?" asked Nicolas. He was trying to sound brave, but it wasn't working.

"That depends on whether or not you've got any food up there," said Armon, breathing heavy as we neared the end of our climb.

Nicolas smiled down at us, and I began to explain why I was lumbering up the side of a cliff on a giant's back with a wolf and a squirrel as my companions. When we reached the top, Armon stood upright and looked down at Nicolas and Pervis. They both looked up, stunned at the size of this creature. Armon sat down, and I broke free of the pouch and ran to embrace Pervis and Nicolas. It became clear right away that Nicolas was only joking about his concern over Armon; he was aware of giants and ogres just as Pervis was, and though it was a surprise to see Armon, it was one they had hoped for.

"This is a development we hadn't expected," said Nicolas, staring in awe at Armon towering over him. "But it's one we're mighty glad for."

"We'll have to be careful about who sees him in these parts," said Pervis. "He'll have to go the long way 'round."

While they spoke I looked at the place where we stood. It was somewhere on the outskirts of Ainsworth, where large boulders sat scattered all along the cliff's edge. We were hidden for the moment.

"Let's drop the rope and get Warvold up here," said Pervis. "There's no time to lose, and he will have thought of our best course of action to handle a giant in our midst."

"What?" I said, surprised. I had been wondering how to tell Pervis and Nicolas that Warvold was alive. Now it seemed that I didn't need to. "How did you know

Warvold was still alive?"

Pervis looked back and forth across the faces before him, and then he pointed at Nicolas.

"He told me."

I looked over at Nicolas. He was fidgeting with his hands, a sheepish look on his face. Since Warvold's "death," I'd felt a special closeness to Nicolas. We'd shared letters, and he'd even visited me twice in the past year.

"You knew all along and you didn't tell me?" I said now. It came out more accusingly than I'd wanted it to, but it was hard to hide that my feelings had been hurt.

"I couldn't tell you, Alexa. It would have been too risky with everything at stake." Nicolas walked over to me and knelt down before continuing. The pleading in his eyes made my heart understand, and immediately I was halfway to forgiving him for keeping his secrets.

"I've known all along about both my mother and my father," he explained. "Many times I battled my father to allow me to rescue Mother. And then, after he told me of his plans to go after her, I begged to go along, or at least to go after him, should he fail. But he is a stubborn man, and he has his own ways. My part in this adventure has been to stay home and keep the kingdom safe, to keep things secret. And it was a good thing, too, or many would have perished in Bridewell these past days."

"He's gone," I said, my voice not much more than a whisper.

A shadow passed over Nicolas's features. "What do you mean?"

"Warvold. He's gone. The boat was blown away as we climbed the cliffs. He's not coming back, at least not for a while."

Nicolas looked at the pouch that hid the last Jocasta hanging around my neck. "That's a bit of bad news I hadn't planned for," he mumbled. "Are you certain he hasn't turned back?"

I rolled the pouch over in my hand and recalled the words I'd heard as we hung from the cliff.

Let them go.

"I'm certain."

Nicolas regained his composure and sat on a large stone before recounting all the events that had occurred while I was away. He had told Pervis to be watchful of me, to tell him the moment I vanished from Bridewell. Having heard this news from my father, Pervis raced to Lunenburg, where Nicolas told him everything he knew (which was a lot more than I'd imagined).

"It was important that we kept things contained to Bridewell to avoid hysteria throughout the kingdom," said Pervis. "I informed my most trusted guards of the danger we might face and sent them far into the Dark Hills to keep watch for anything moving in our direction."

"It's a very good thing we're such a timid people in times such as these," said Nicolas. "The legend of the giants has always been something of a mystery to the people of Bridewell Common. It's talked about more in Ainsworth, where people like such stories. Still, there is a healthy fear of all things outside our kingdom, and a deep longing for the past when my father was still here."

He took a deep breath before continuing. "When we received word from the guards that Grindall and his giants were sleeping in the hills only a day's journey away, I called a meeting in the town square of all the people who remained in Bridewell. Many were already gone. As you know, summer is the time when most are out gathering books for repair. But there were still at least five hundred who remained. We simply had to get them out without alarming the other towns of the approaching danger."

"Ogres," I said. "You called them giants, the beasts that travel with Grindall. Armon is the only giant that remains. The rest are ogres."

Nicolas looked at me strangely, as if I'd made mention of something of little importance. But it was important to me.

Nicolas went on to tell us that he'd revealed to the townspeople that as Warvold's only son he'd been left with a message from his father. The people, who had once been so enamored of Warvold and who still missed him so much, were very interested in what this message might say.

Now Nicolas pulled a scrap of paper from his vest pocket and read us the note that Warvold had left, the same note he'd read to the people in Bridewell only two days before.

I have given this message to my son, Nicolas, who you can trust. If it is being read to you, then something has happened that requires your immediate action. There is a danger approaching, a danger that is hard to explain and best left unknown. It is a danger that will only last a few days. Then it will pass through and will never be seen or heard from again.

I must ask you to leave Bridewell and go to the neighboring towns in our kingdom until Nicolas summons you back again. Trust me this last time and leave until this danger passes through. Tell no one of this peril, for it will only cause panic throughout the kingdom and bring people where they should not go.

Again I say: Trust me once more and the danger will pass. It will be a fleeting shadow over Bridewell that you never need worry over . . . as long as you leave as I have instructed.

Warvold

"It wasn't very hard to convince them," Pervis interjected, his protective nature coming out in the way he spoke. "This was a message from Warvold, who'd taken care of them and envisioned everything around them. The idea of leaving to avoid whatever was coming unnerved them, but the idea of staying to fight whatever it was sounded far worse. They were quick in their packing, and they promised to keep it secret. There were a few travelers from outside the city, from Turlock and

Ainsworth, and these I had to pull aside and do some extra convincing."

Pained, Pervis reached his conclusion: "Bridewell is empty but for Grindall and his ogres."

My cherished town of Bridewell was overrun. All my favorite places — the library, the chambers, the tunnels — they were no longer ours. I thought of Yipes trapped with those awful creatures, wondering if someone would come to save him.

"We need to go there," I said.

Pervis and Nicolas looked as though they hoped Warvold might have left a plan in my keeping. While that wasn't the case, I was overcome with concern for Yipes, and I knew we had to rescue him. I had been working on a plan of my own, a plan that meant we'd have to go to Bridewell.

"Warvold and I spoke on the boat, and I know what we must do," I said. Pervis and Nicolas seemed to perk up at this remark. Armon, Murphy, and Odessa remained at my side, quietly listening as things unfolded. It was true I'd spoken to Warvold, so it was only half a lie, but I felt terrible having to tell it.

I continued, "Yipes is held captive by Grindall and the ogres. It would be a tragic mistake to leave him there. The first thing we must do is rescue him."

There was a new look of intensity from the both of them, especially Pervis. I had a plan and our dear friend was imprisoned by our enemy. The motivation they needed had been set in place.

As morning turned to afternoon, we began talking about how we might hide a giant on the road to Bridewell.

CHAPTER 8

RETURN TO THE TUNNELS

We decided to stay in the Dark Hills while the light of day remained. It was the only way to keep Armon at a safe distance from those who might see him in Ainsworth and Lunenburg. I was very pleased to find that Pervis and Nicolas had brought two horses with them. Murphy and I sat atop one with Pervis in front while Nicolas rode on the other. Armon and Odessa walked. It made for a much easier day of trudging through the Dark Hills. At one point, I walked alongside Odessa alone and we talked of many things — of Sherwin and Darius, the woods and the mountains, and even my secret plans. She was a curious creature, quiet and secretive, not unlike her mate, Darius. I hadn't seen Squire all morning, and I wondered if she'd stayed with Warvold and the others on the *Warwick Beacon*.

Later I talked with Pervis and Nicolas, wondering how they'd known we would arrive as we did at the cliffs. As I might have guessed, my mother had sent word when Renny arrived in Lathbury. Silas Hardy, the mail carrier and friend to my father, had been sent to Bridewell with a message that the *Warwick Beacon* was coming around the bend and could appear at the appointed place anytime. It was all a part of Warvold's elaborate plan — a plan that seemed to grow more mysterious with each passing revelation. I wished then that I could have a mind like his, one that could look so far ahead and think of everything so far in advance. It was a brilliance reserved for someone much older than me.

As evening approached we found ourselves closing in on the walls of Bridewell, the aboveground tunnels of underbrush before us. They snaked all along the ground, gnarly and brown, filled with thorns and tangled branches. It was hard to imagine Armon fitting inside the narrow passageways. We walked along an edge of thick brush until we were somewhere directly between Castalia and Bridewell. If Grindall had walked a straight line from his fallen Dark Tower to Bridewell, he'd have entered here. We discovered without too much surprise that the ogres had ignored the tunnels. They'd walked right over them, cutting and slashing with their mighty swords as they went, so the path lay straight and true right up to the walls of Bridewell itself. It was a long way off, far enough that I could only make the idea of the walls in my mind, but I felt sure that somewhere off in the distance an ogre was standing at the tower looking all around for intruders.

We walked the horses west a hundred yards, and Pervis began to tie them to a sad-looking, broken-down tree.

"That might not be such a good idea, unless you want them to be stuck out here," I said.

Pervis held the reins and seemed ready to protest before offering a quiet response.

"We're not coming back this way, are we?" he said.

"I'm afraid not," I told him. "We must try to rescue Yipes tonight. After that, we'll be racing for the Sly Field."

Nicolas took both the reins from Pervis in one hand and patted the horses on their noses.

"They know the way home to Lunenburg," Nicolas said. "I'm quite sure they'll find their way by morning." To both horses, he warned, "Stay together now; don't run off in different directions." Then he came around to the side of the larger of the two, and whispered, "She'll follow you." He slapped the horse and off it ran, the smaller one racing behind in the direction of Lunenburg.

As we stood looking into the maze of tunnels that remained in the brush, a thought occurred to me. It was the strangest thing that I hadn't thought of it at all and no one had mentioned it all day.

"Where's my father?" I asked, suddenly concerned for him.

An awkward silence filled the air while Pervis and Nicolas looked at each other as if to decide who would answer my question.

"He was sure you'd return to Bridewell," Pervis finally said. "I tried to make him leave, but he wouldn't."

I pictured ogres climbing over the walls, finding my father alone and helpless.

"You can't have left him there to die?" I pleaded.

Pervis seemed to liven up at my comment.

"You vastly underestimate your father, Alexa. He's not only resourceful, but he knows Bridewell and all its secret places quite well. When we left he was already belowground in the secret tunnels, awaiting your arrival. I told him I'd never bring you back here with those monsters around the place, but he was quite sure you would return whether I liked it or not."

"Did anyone stay with him, or is he all alone?" I asked.

"I'm afraid he's alone, Alexa. He was very persuasive about making sure all my guards were sent away. This was his decision, and he didn't want anyone else put in harm's way."

For the first time I felt regret for my actions. I'd put him in terrible danger.

Nicolas spoke as if he'd read my mind.

"There are some things you have yet to understand, Alexa — things that I think will become clear in the coming days. But you can be sure of one thing: James Daley is doing exactly what he should be doing right now, as are the rest of us, including you."

Murphy jumped into my arms and said to me, "Just think, Alexa. You'll see your father again on this very night!"

Pervis seemed very interested in Murphy, and he walked closer.

"I've been listening to the two of you all day. Is it really true what I've been told? Can you understand what this little creature is saying with all his squeaks and sounds?"

Murphy twitched and jumped and carried on in my arms.

"He says he was digging around in your bag earlier and spied a bag of nuts," I said. "He wants to have some and asks if you might kindly hand them over."

Pervis looked on in astonishment, removed the bag of nuts, and pulled out a nice large one.

"Here you go, little fellow," he said. "That ought to keep you busy for a while." As Murphy chomped away, Pervis shook his head. "Amazing. I thought Nicolas was making a grand joke with me. You really *can* talk to animals, then."

"Let's keep that a secret between just the few of us, shall we?" I said.

Pervis nodded as he crunched on a handful of nuts.

"I can't wait to get to Bridewell," I said, thinking only of my father and Yipes. "Another hour and we can safely move in the dark."

I looked at Armon. His hulking presence cast a shadow big enough for us all to stand in. I knew there was still the black swarm to contend with. I looked into the sky, listening instinctively for the sound of leathery wings on the wind, but there was nothing to be heard.

The hour before dark passed with the making of plans as we sat in a circle eating and drinking, gaining strength for the long night ahead. Nicolas had brought bread and fresh-cooked meat along with a small leather bag full of hard candies — something I hadn't enjoyed in quite a while. It was especially pleasing to watch Murphy eat the candy, his eyes bulging with delight, the sugar sending him into a fit of talking and darting about.

"Is he always like this?" asked Pervis.

We watched as Murphy sniffed and dashed all around us in a fit of activity, then ran up the side of Armon and darted between his shoulders.

"Not always, but most of the time, yes," said Armon, a pleasant air of affection in his voice.

It was decided that Armon was too big to hide or fit into the tunnels as we went about our business in Bridewell. He would travel around in secret and meet us at a place I knew of in the forest. It was somewhere from my past, on the other side of

Bridewell — the meadow cast with moonlight where Ander the bear made his home and the forest council met. Armon said he knew how to find it. I only hoped we'd rescue Yipes so he could help me remember how to get there.

I watched Armon as he walked away, sliding back into the darkness from where he'd come to save us only days before. I hadn't realized how comforting his presence was, and a terrible emptiness filled my heart as he disappeared. I wished then that we'd come up with some other plan in which he could stay with us.

"We must be getting on," said Odessa. "We've been resting here long enough."

She strode into the tunnel before us, and the rest of us followed. It wasn't long before Murphy was well in front, scampering from side to side down the pathway.

"He's a good scout," I said. "He'll tell us if danger is lurking ahead."

As it turned out, we had no trouble along the pathway and before long arrived at a clearing, the walls of Bridewell visible by the firelight from the lookouts. There was a stench in the air, a rotten smell rising on the wind. There was a little more than a half-moon in the sky, and I could make out the shape of something large standing on the nearest tower on the wall. One of the remaining ogres was keeping watch.

"The underground tunnel we must enter is that way." I pointed to my right. In the faint moonlight I could see where it was, only a hundred feet away.

"We'll have to go slowly, in the open, to reach it," I continued. "But there's something I didn't tell you before."

Pervis and Nicolas looked at each other as if they might have expected me to say such a thing.

"The two of you will have to wait here with Odessa," I told them. "The entrance to the tunnel is very small. Only Murphy and I will fit."

"I won't allow it," said Pervis, suddenly acting as though I'd tricked him into bringing me to this spot. "I promised your father I wouldn't let you return here, so I'm already in trouble. I can't let you go alone, Alexa. If something happens to you, I'll never forgive myself."

I had expected this response and had planned my answer carefully as we walked through the night. I was about to tell a truly awful lie, one that I thought might be my undoing. But I knew of no other way to rescue Yipes than to sneak back into Bridewell through the tiny opening he and

I had used to escape on our way to Castalia.

"Do you know what's inside this pouch?" I asked Pervis, holding the hidden Jocasta out to him.

"Only that what you carry is very important, and that you alone must carry it," he answered.

"This is the very last Jocasta. It's what makes it possible for me to understand what Murphy and Odessa say — and it's also what makes it possible for me to hear another voice as well, a voice on the wind."

"Elyon?" Pervis whispered in disbelief. I nodded, and then I told my lie.

"Elyon has told me to enter the city through a hole Yipes and I used to sneak away. As I said before, it's too small for any of us but Murphy and me. So I *must* leave the rest of you behind."

"What?" whispered Pervis, a bit louder than he should have. We all crouched down in the bushes and watched the tower, but nothing seemed to stir near the flame on the wall.

"I'm sorry, Pervis. I really am — but we have to do this the way I've been told."

He shook his head back and forth and looked to Nicolas for support, but it seemed as though I'd convinced Warvold's son that this was the only way.

"James will be down there waiting for her," said Nicolas. "He'll be angry with you, but Alexa will have him for protection. I'm just glad Grindall knows nothing of the tunnels below the city."

"Couldn't I fit in that hole?" asked Pervis. "I'm not that much bigger than you are, Alexa."

This was something I hadn't thought of, and it got me to wondering.

"I don't think you'll fit, but I can't be completely sure about it."

"I'm going with you. I want to at least try."

I knew by looking at Nicolas that he would never fit, and Odessa was such a large wolf I couldn't imagine her making it inside. But Pervis was a small man, and he was very determined to protect me. It was unlikely, but I had to allow him an attempt.

"You wait here," Pervis ordered Nicolas and Odessa. "If I can't make it in I'll be back in a few minutes. If I fit inside . . ." Pervis paused, thinking. "Well, I suppose you ought to wait here and see if we return with James and Yipes or not."

It seemed that the planning might go on for a while — and we didn't have any time to be sitting in the Dark Hills figuring things out. I started walking quietly toward the hole. Murphy jumped out in front, darting from side to side. Pervis whispered my name, but I kept going, and sure enough he was right behind me by the time I reached the hole and looked down inside.

"There it is," I said. "I'm going in first. If you get wedged like a cork I don't want to be stuck out here trying to get you out." It was a modest little joke, but it made Murphy laugh and laugh. I was reminded again that I must never give him sweets.

I followed Murphy into the small hole in the ground and slithered down to the bottom where the boards had been replaced. I listened carefully and, hearing nothing, pushed out the boards with my hands and dropped into the room. There was no one in the room, and it was pitch dark. I realized too late that I'd made a grave error. There was no light, and I'd brought none with me.

"Pervis!" I whispered, afraid that Grindall or one of the ogres might have discovered this place. It would be hard for an ogre to get around in the tunnels, but not impossible if they'd found another way in.

I groped around the room and listened

as Pervis struggled to make his way down the narrow tunnel. I was too late, since he'd already begun his descent down into the room. If he got stuck it would be a long, dark night trying to get him out.

"Oh, dear." It was Pervis, and I had the distinct feeling that he'd gotten himself lodged in the tunnel. I put my arms in and tried to grasp for his hands. I was able to touch his fingers but only barely, so I couldn't pull him into the room. He was indeed trapped.

I turned and sat against the wall, where Murphy jumped on my lap. I couldn't see him — I couldn't see anything. Pervis was stuck in the hole, and I couldn't help him or find my way around. Things weren't going very well, and as I sat there wondering what to do, things managed to get even worse.

From somewhere down a distant tunnel, a light was coming my way, flickering and bobbing back and forth as if whatever carried it were clumsily racing through. Had Grindall known of this place all along and expected my arrival?

It was so dark that I couldn't see Murphy as he dashed from my lap and sniffed the air.

"We'd better hide," he said. "Something

smells terrible . . . and it's coming this way."

I felt the goose bumps rising on my scrawny arms. I yelped quietly as Murphy brushed against my legs and scampered back into my lap. We were trapped, and we couldn't even see to hide. All we could make out was the light bouncing miserably on the walls in the distance, coming closer.

CHAPTER 9

OUT OF THE DARKNESS

"Pervis," I whispered, "you've got to get out! You've got to go back."

As the light came closer I was able to see a little of the space around me. The board we'd pushed out into the room lay next to me. Seeing it, I realized there was only one place we could go that might hide us from whatever was coming our way.

"I'm really stuck, Alexa." It was Pervis, whispering from the hole.

"It's all right; just stay quiet. We're coming in with you."

"What?"

There was no time to answer him as I picked up the board and stood it up next to the hole. Murphy jumped in first.

"Come on, Alexa, hurry!" Murphy squeaked.

I got down on my hands and knees with my feet facing the hole. It was awkward, but I was able to back myself inside, feet first. Then, lying there, I picked up the board and pulled it back into place over the hole just as the light reached the room.

Pervis was so close that my feet were right in his face, and I had the feeling that I was probably pushing my heel into his nose. Murphy was doing his best to stay still down near my legs, but sitting still was very hard for him. His twitches tickled the backs of my knees, and I had to struggle not to move my legs in response.

I couldn't see anything in the room with the board back in place, and I began to worry as my grip on the board lessened and I slid forward little by little toward the room. Murphy squeezed up onto my back and made his way up next to my head, where he sniffed.

"No worries," he whispered into my ear. He leaned into the board and pushed it free into the room. I slid halfway out of the hole, staring at the ground in front of me, waiting for an ogre to attack.

Two arms grabbed hold of me by the middle and lifted me out of the hole and into the air. I opened my eyes and stared in disbelief.

It was my father, a big grin on his face. He pulled me into a warm embrace.

"Father!" I said. But that was all I could muster. I simply felt around his large arms and pulled free to look at him once more. It was really him, looking at me with wonder in his eyes, so happy to find that I was safe and unharmed.

"It's so very good to see you, Alexa," he said as he set me down and bent on one knee. "I've been thinking the most terrible thoughts these past days. But you're all right after all."

"At least for the moment I am," I said. I didn't have the heart to tell him I was afraid there was quite a lot more for me to do before I'd consider myself safe again.

"What would be the odds of someone helping me get free?" It was Pervis, still struggling to remove himself from where he was wedged solidly in the hole.

"It's Pervis — he's stuck in there." I pointed to the hole, and my father got up and poked his head inside the dark opening.

"Is that you in there, Pervis? All those extra helpings of potatoes finally got the best of you."

"Very funny," answered Pervis.

"I really ought to leave you in there,

since you deliberately disobeyed my order not to bring Alexa back here."

"She made me do it!" he yelled desperately.

My father looked over at me. "It's true she can be very persuasive. Still, I think I'll leave you there awhile. Maybe it will harden your resolve in case you're tempted to disobey me again."

My father was clowning with him. I began to feel sorry for Pervis, all wedged in there as he was.

"Father, Yipes is in Bridewell. He is a prisoner of Grindall, and we've come to save him. That's the only reason we've come back."

This remark seemed to sober my father's playfulness. He immediately put his arms into the hole, took hold of Pervis's hands, and pulled hard.

"Ooooowww!" Pervis yelled.

My father let him go and peered into the hole.

"You really are stuck, aren't you?"

"I think I moved a little when you pulled just then," Pervis answered. "Try it again."

My father grabbed Pervis by the hands once more and pulled with all his might. Pervis yelped as he came tumbling out of the hole and landed on top of my father, the two of them covered in dirt on the floor of the tunnel.

"Thank you! I'll never disobey you again."

"Get off me, Pervis," ordered my father.

Pervis was quick to jump free of my father and offer to help him up. They both brushed off, and the three of us stood there in the weak light of the tunnel with Murphy skittering around the room.

"How did that squirrel get in here?" asked my father.

Murphy squeaked and squeaked. He was apologizing, saying he'd smelled something that wasn't right and thought it was an ogre. As it turns out it was just my father, who hadn't washed in many days and smelled a bit ripe himself.

"It's all right, Murphy. I might have made the same mistake myself," I said.

"Why are you talking to that rodent?" said my father.

"It's a long story, but he says you smell bad and you need to take a bath."

My father bent down and looked into Murphy's face.

"Can we talk about it later, please?" I begged. "We need to find Yipes before it's too late."

My father seemed to take this as a reasonable suggestion, though he remained wary of Murphy and curious about what was going on.

"Fine, then. Have your fun if you want to, but you're not going up there. It's far too dangerous with those ogres around the place. I'll go."

I wasn't sure what I should do. I couldn't let him get anywhere near Victor Grindall. It was far too dangerous.

He'll go by way of the courtyard. You must let him.

It was the voice, once again telling me something I didn't want to hear. How could I send my own father into a place where monsters waited — monsters that had already taken John Christopher from me?

"We'll both go," said Pervis, shifting his eyes between me and my father. "The two of us can do it while Alexa waits down here for us."

My father looked at Pervis in the gloom of the tunnel, and the two of them seemed to agree that it was the only way.

"I came into the tunnels through the guard's entrance hidden in the courtyard," my father told us. "I've been hiding down here since Grindall arrived, so I don't know where they are. We'll go back the way I came in and scout around for where they might be keeping Yipes. My bet is they've put him in one of the prison cells in the basement of Renny Lodge. We should be able to sneak down there at this hour and look around."

"What if there's an ogre guarding the basement?" I asked.

Pervis and my father looked at each other and shrugged.

"We'll have to cross that bridge when we come to it," said my father. "If we can't rescue him at least we'll know where he is. That's a first step."

My father led us through the tunnels and into a room where he'd stored up some provisions and another lamp. He lit the lamp and trimmed it low, then gave me a very firm look.

"You stay here, Alexa. There's nothing you can do but get yourself into trouble if you try to follow us."

I nodded and sat down on his makeshift bed, hopeful that they would find Yipes somewhere within Bridewell without encountering ogres.

Pervis and my father took one of the two lamps, along with swords my father had brought down with him.

As they turned to go, I said, "Father?"

"Yes?" He turned back and looked at me.

"Please be careful. If you even see an ogre, run for your life. They're impossible to stop." I knew the ogres could be defeated, but I wanted Pervis and my father as far away from danger as I could get them. If my father knew that a knife to the top of the head could kill an ogre, he'd waste no time in trying it.

"There's nothing to worry about. I've got Pervis to protect me," my father said. Pervis took this as the joke it was and gave my father a sour look. They began walking again. Soon it was very quiet in the room; even Murphy sat still as a statue. The very air seemed to stop cold.

Go to the library by your usual way.

I'd had a feeling this was going to happen — that I would hear the voice again, guiding me to a familiar place. All roads seemed to lead back to the library, and somehow I knew that rescuing Yipes was my task, not my father's.

I hesitated a moment and closed my eyes. It was dark and quiet inside my head, and I realized then how tired I was. I shook my head and opened my eyes, rubbing them with my hands before standing up.

"Murphy," I said, "are you ready for another adventure?"

"Always ready, Alexa," he replied.

I picked up the lamp and began walking to where the stairs led up into the library, behind my favorite old chair, a place where I had enjoyed so many lazy days of reading and resting. Murphy ran ahead, scouting the way, and I was lost in my thoughts, trying to remember all the nooks and crannies of the old library, the rooms in Renny Lodge, the places I could hide and where I thought Grindall might be.

The smoking room. The room with the giant wall of stone and the flames licking in the grand fireplace. The velvety couches and the high ceilings. That's where he would be plotting and planning, his awful ogres milling around in the shadows near him, waiting for me to come to him and give him the stone.

But where would he put Yipes?

CHAPTER 10

THE LIBRARY

There had been a long walk through the tunnels, winding this way and that, before we found ourselves at the bottom of the ladder, looking up into the shadows. I took a long, quiet moment to consider the day's events. The questions were coming faster than answers, and my head was swimming with anxiety. Where were Warvold and my other friends? What was my father encountering? Where would this adventure lead? Where was Yipes? Standing there at the bottom of the ladder I soon realized that the only way I would find the answers to any of my questions was to keep on with the journey. Stopping only left me worn out with my own thoughts. And so I climbed.

We reached the top of the ladder. I was about to open the trapdoor that led into the library. Murphy sat happily on my shoulder, wondering what might be waiting for us inside.

"Are you ready to bite some ogres?" I said.

"I can hardly wait." He was a silly little squirrel, but he certainly was brave.

"Here we come, Yipes," I whispered. "Prepare to be rescued by a fur ball and a lanky thirteen-year-old."

I turned the latch, and it clicked ever so quietly. Then the door swung open into the darkness of the tunnel. It no longer squeaked when it opened — Pervis had seen to that last summer when he'd discovered it and forbade me from ever using it again. Though he kept the key and never used the secret door, he couldn't help making the rusty hinges right again.

My favorite chair remained in its usual place, with its back pushed up against the trapdoor, concealing the opening to all my adventures. It smelled a little ogrish inside, but not so much that I thought we might find them sitting around reading books. This was probably the last place they would choose to spend time.

I placed my hands against the back of the chair and braced myself, ready to push it out of the way so we could enter the library.

"Wait," whispered Murphy. He was right next to my ear, so I knew immediately to remain still. Something was near.

A black leather-booted foot hit the old wooden floor of the library, then another. The feet had been propped up on the box where I'd propped up my own feet so often. The boots were not huge, like those of an ogre, and they had silver rings that clanged as they hit the floorboards. A book was placed heavily on the wood box in front of the chair, and whoever it was stood, advanced to the one window in the room, and grumbled. A chain rattled on the floor as he went.

"Where is she? Where is that insolent girl with my stone?"

It was Victor Grindall who'd been sitting in my chair, reading my books, and kicking up his feet on my wooden box. I was very glad then that Pervis had oiled the hinges on the trapdoor! Murphy and I stayed perfectly still, waiting to see what Grindall would do.

I listened as he slumped back down in the chair and picked up his book once more, propping up his feet as he flipped through the pages.

"She must show herself by tomorrow or I'll have to throw you out the window," Grindall threatened, his wicked voice echoing off the walls in the library. "That might not be so bad after all. I'm sick and tired of dragging you around."

"You should throw me out now. She's not coming here. She knows better than to risk it." It was Yipes! He was in the room. It sounded as though he was sitting on the windowsill.

Grindall laughed out loud, a cackle of a laugh that angered me so much I wanted to push away the chair and take him on. The chain rattled on the floor as Grindall played with it in his hand.

"Oh, she'll come. I have little doubt of that. And when she does, I'll kill you both." He laughed again and seemed to settle into the chair. I wished I could see Yipes and know that he was unharmed.

"The two of them must be chained together." It was Murphy, whispering in my ear again. "Why don't I sneak under the chair and see what sort of shape our friend is in?"

This seemed like a good idea. There was plenty of room for Murphy to crawl under the chair and catch a glimpse of Yipes at the windowsill. I took him in my hand and set him down carefully on the floor of the library. At first he hesitated, but then he crept ever so slowly to the edge of the chair and looked out in the direction of the windowsill.

"She has many allies," said Yipes, "some

large and some small, and all with more bravery than you can muster from your ogres."

Yipes was signaling us with his carefully chosen words that he'd seen Murphy.

"Shut up!" answered Grindall. "If you can't keep quiet while I'm reading I'll shackle you to an ogre instead. When they get hungry they don't bother to ask if they can eat what's chained to their leg."

Murphy was back on my shoulder twitching and fidgeting, trying to stay calm and quiet as he whispered in my ear.

"He's sitting on the windowsill in a cage that's chained to Grindall. The cage has a big lock on it. I don't see how we can get him free."

As Murphy said this, the sound of giant footsteps filled the library. The very floor shook and creaked as something approached. The smell outran the beast, and my nostrils filled with that wretched odor of rotting flesh. An ogre was approaching, and he seemed to be in a rush.

When the ogre rounded the corner I could see his huge feet approaching Grindall, trapped in worn leather boots. The feet alone were enough to scare me.

"What is it now?" Grindall asked, annoyed.

The ogre grunted and wheezed, the

gurgling sound of his voice a terrible reminder of what would happen to Armon if the black swarm ever found him.

"Interesting," said Grindall. "You're sure you smelled something? Something not quite right?"

The ogre spoke excitedly again as Grindall's feet came crashing off the wooden box onto the floor in front of me.

"She is here then, in the lodge, looking for her little friend," said Grindall. "Well, let's make sure she finds him, shall we?"

Grindall stood, and I heard the chain rattling, a key being inserted into a lock.

"I'm going to look for her, and when I find her I'll bring her here," said Grindall. The ogre seemed to be wrapping the chain around his massive waist. The lock was clamped shut once more.

"Don't eat him! I want her to observe as we put an end to her friend."

Grindall stomped away into the library, and his footsteps were soon lost in the distance. The ogre sniffed the air all around him while I quietly closed the trapdoor, sealing us in. I stepped down the ladder seven or eight rungs and waited, the low-burning lamp at my side.

From where I stood lower in the tunnel I could still hear the ogre smelling the air, searching for something that did not seem quite right. I listened as he grabbed hold of the chair and thrust it forward out of his way. It sounded as though the chair had tipped over and probably lay on its front on the wooden floor of the library. The chains rattled and the ogre grunted, but he seemed to accept that nothing lay behind the chair but a wall. Next he trudged over to the windowsill and took an interest in Yipes. I hoped he wouldn't rip open the cage and make a late dinner out of him.

I climbed back up the ladder and listened at the secret door, not sure what to do. I wondered where Pervis and my father were, if they were safe or if they'd been captured. It was hard to imagine a more perilous feeling than the one I had hanging there from the ladder. I wanted only to be home by the sea, mending books, my world put back together again.

With the chair thrown away from the wall, I couldn't open the door again without being seen. I was at a dead end, my friend locked in a cage and chained to an ogre, an eager squirrel my only help. As I stood listening, it sounded as though the ogre sat down on the floor of the library near the window, grunting and sniffing, his breath labored in what sounded like a wet sponge of lungs.

Yipes began to taunt the beast as he sat against the wall, which I couldn't understand. Didn't he know that he might be eaten or stomped on if he enraged the ogre?

"I have many friends you know, more than Grindall can keep track of."

The ogre only gargled and grunted at Yipes, as if to tell him to be quiet.

"Some of my friends are small, but some are *large,* as big as you."

The ogre rumbled more fiercely now and banged his mighty hand on the stone wall. I wished I could see what was going on.

"There are even secret places, places you know nothing about. Hiding places in this very library."

What was Yipes doing? It was as though he were trying to give us up, to drive us away so that we wouldn't get hurt. I could only imagine that he wished us to leave and carry out what remained of our plan without him. He had to know that once this close I could never leave him to die at the hands of Victor Grindall.

The ogre was back on his feet, grumbling loudly and shaking the cage at the sill, no doubt battering Yipes around inside. Then the ogre laughed hideously, a gurgling sort of laugh that turned into a cough. I heard the chain clanging against the wall and knew in an instant that the ogre had dropped Yipes off the edge where he dangled from the chain in the cage. The ogre was having a bit of fun, swinging poor Yipes back and forth in the night air.

"I wouldn't do that if I were you. Grindall won't be happy if you harm me," said Yipes. I could barely hear him through the trapdoor and the stone of the wall. "Besides, with your back turned, someone might *open a trapdoor* and jump out after you!"

What was he thinking? Could he mean for me to open the door for some unthinkable reason? I couldn't understand what Yipes was up to, and I stood on the ladder completely baffled by the unseen events unfolding only a few feet away.

The ogre yanked on the chain — pulling Yipes back into the room — and slammed the cage back down on the sill, shaking it mercilessly.

"Trust me!" Yipes called out.

The ogre was becoming angrier and angrier as I reached my shaking hand out for the latch and took hold of it. I turned it just so and I heard the quiet click of metal against metal.

And then I opened the door.

CHAPTER 11

THE DANGLING CHAIN

As the secret door opened, the air from the library escaped into the tunnel. It was an evil smell, so thick it was like a dark cloud poisoning everything it touched. I saw what I had previously only imagined: The chair was flipped onto its side, pushed into the corner. The ogre stood at the windowsill shaking the cage that held Yipes. The chain was wrapped around the ogre's waist and secured with a lock, the other end attached to the cage where Yipes was bouncing inside.

"You see there," said Yipes, pointing in my direction as he was thrown all around inside the small cage. "I told you there were secret places."

Unbelievable! I began to think Yipes had gone mad, driven crazy by the long days of companionship with Victor Grindall and his ogres.

At first the ogre thought it was a trick and wouldn't look at me, but his curiosity quickly overcame him. The ogre turned and looked at me, my head and shoulders in plain view, and for a moment he seemed not to believe what he was seeing. He shook his head as he'd shook the cage, gobs of thick drool spewing into the room. I was frozen with fear, unable to move, as I watched Murphy dart out between us and onto the sill.

The ogre paid Murphy no attention as he turned his back on Yipes and cackled in my direction. Then he started for me, a grand prize for his master within his reach.

As he turned, the chain followed him like a slithering black snake, winding behind him where it ended at the cage. The window where the ogre had stood was suddenly filled with a great shadow, but it was quickly blocked from my view as the ogre bent over and reached down his awful hand to grab hold of me. I was too afraid to think, too afraid to try to escape. I simply waited for the ogre to pull me into the room and take me to Grindall. A familiar feeling of hopelessness and failure flooded me as the last Jocasta was about to be taken from me and put into the hands of my enemy. I could already hear Victor Grindall's laugh echoing through Renny Lodge.

What happened next was mostly a blur, something I felt even more than I saw. It happened very quickly and without warning. I heard the sound of breaking chains and the cage falling to the floor, which made the ogre turn from me just as he was about to put his hand on my shoulder and drag me into the room. The ogre was pulled back violently toward the window by the chain wrapped around his waist. He made an awful sound when the chain jerked tight and pulled him off his feet, the sickly air and liquid flying from his lungs in a great snorting howl. The ogre was stunned but not destroyed, and as I looked on in astonishment I saw that it was Armon who had come through the large open window. He took hold of the ogre and threw him against the wall, then dragged him to the window and threw him out.

Armon looked back at me for a moment and smiled, then he, too, headed for the window to face the ogre outside. I jumped from my perch on the ladder into the room as Armon disappeared. Advancing to the window, I watched as Armon finished off the ogre and ran for the wall. Then I heard not one but two terrible sounds.

The black swarm was coming from somewhere overhead, and in the night sky I watched as Armon scaled the ivy-covered wall, trying to outrun the furious sound of bat wings in the air. He was so fast it took him only a moment to find his way to the top. He took no time to look back at us as he dropped over the other side and was gone. I listened as the bats came overhead. I watched the stars disappear, the night turned completely black by the mass of dark creatures. They flew over the wall and after Armon. I shuddered with fear for him.

I had little time to worry about this, however, for another noise came almost at the same time as the black swarm. It was Grindall entering the library with ogres in tow, and his voice was filled with rage.

Yipes, sitting in the cage at my feet, hastily said, "Alexa, now might be a good time to make our exit."

"What shall we do? We're trapped!" I said.

"Take hold of the cage and carry me into the tunnel. Quickly now!"

I did as I was told, carrying the heavy

cage with the broken end of the chain rattling behind me until I reached the opening. I ran in front of the cage and through the secret door, grabbed hold of the ladder, and yanked on the chain, unsure whether or not I could hold the weight of Yipes dangling from one arm. Murphy, holding on to the outside of the cage with his claws, came right into the tunnel with Yipes.

The cage fell free into the darkness beneath me, and I yelped in pain when its full weight found the end of the falling chain and nearly jerked me clean off the ladder into the air. The chain slipped quickly through my fingers for seven or eight links, then slowed as I tightened my grip, and finally stopped with Yipes dangling back and forth below me.

It took every ounce of strength I had not to let go. Murphy jumped from the cage and held on to the ladder as the chain started slipping slowly through my fingers again. Yipes was dangling high above the ground, and I was close to dropping him.

I watched and listened as things unfolded out of my control all around me. The secret door was still wide open, revealing us to anyone who might look my way. Grindall and the ogres were about to turn the corner, but I couldn't close the door — I held the ladder with one hand and the cage with the other. I was helpless to conceal our escape. At the same moment that Grindall came around the corner, Murphy reached the top of the ladder. He jumped to the trapdoor — which swung free inside the tunnel — then pushed with his tail against the wall. Murphy held on to the back of the little door, and when he pushed with his tail the door swung shut. I watched through the last crack of light as Grindall and the ogres came fuming around the corner.

I tried desperately not to make a sound, but the chain was starting to dig into my hand as it kept sliding slowly through my fingers. I was left with about a foot of chain links yet to go as Yipes hung four or five feet below me. I could hear Grindall and the ogres cursing and yelling in a terrible fury, trying to figure out what had happened. Yipes was gone, and an ogre was dead outside. It gave me some pleasure and renewed strength to think of how angry Grindall must have been as he looked at the scene before him.

"What's happened?" he screamed. "I don't understand!"

He was yelling into the night sky through

the window. I'd never heard him so completely outraged.

"It's that girl. It's Alexa," he said, his raging replaced by a malevolent, slow drawl. "But how?"

I couldn't hold the chain any longer. It began to slip through my fingers faster than before, only inches left until it slid out of my hand entirely and Yipes fell with a crash that would surely alert Grindall to the secret door.

"Hold on, Alexa," whispered Murphy. "Only a little longer."

"Search this library!" shouted Grindall. "Tear it all down book by book if you have to. If you can smell them they must be hiding in here somewhere."

I was at once relieved and heartbroken as I heard the shelves start to fall, books flying everywhere, the ogres tearing my wonderful library to pieces. As I finally lost my grip on the chain, I listened to it free-fall through the air, a light clanging in the air around me, and then a great crash as Yipes hit the dirt floor and the chain rattled behind the cage like a dinner bell.

"Stop!" yelled Grindall. I was already moving down the stairs, quietly making my escape with Murphy perched on my shoulder. The sound of ogres walking around above was like a terrible, thundering sky, their weight almost too much for the old wooden floor of the library to hold.

"Stop moving, you fools!" said Grindall. "I heard something."

All was quiet above as I reached the bottom of the ladder and held the lamp over the cage. Yipes was still locked inside, though the cage itself was badly bent on one corner.

"That hurt," whispered Yipes.

"Shhhhhh," said Murphy in response, and the three of us sat with only the sound of our breath between us.

"Back to work with you! Keep looking." Grindall had tired of listening, and the ogres were tearing at the shelves once more.

"We'd better get moving," said Murphy.

I set the lamp on top of the cage and took hold of the chain, dragging Yipes on the floor. It was hard work — very slow going — but it wasn't long before the sounds of the library being torn apart were only a whisper somewhere behind us.

"You're heavy for such a little man," I said, huffing as I stopped to rest. Yipes had his fingers through the cage to hold the lamp so it wouldn't topple over. I noticed then that Murphy was doing his best to push the cage from behind.

"Thank you for the help, Murphy," I said. It was unlikely that he was actually doing much good, but I had to commend his effort.

"You saved me," said Yipes, tears welling up in his eyes. He was looking back and forth between the two of us.

"Think nothing of it," said Murphy. "It was quite a good time we had doing it."

I smiled and allowed myself a moment of peace knowing that Yipes — although locked in a cage I couldn't get him out of — was unharmed and in good spirits. My fingers were small enough that I could easily fit them into the cage, and I poked them in. He touched his tiny fingers to mine, and we both knew the gesture was — at least for now — the closest thing to a welcoming embrace we would be allowed.

"We have to get out of here as fast as we can," I said. "I fear Grindall won't stop until he's found this place."

As I took hold of the chain and began pulling again, something occurred to me — even if I could drag Yipes all the way to the ladder that led to the outside, I wouldn't be able to get Yipes up and out of the tunnel. This was beginning to seem like a typical day — Yipes in a cage, the library ripped apart, the fate of Armon, my father, and Pervis unknown . . . and a long, hard journey ahead of me.

CHAPTER 12

ESCAPE FROM THE TUNNELS

I hadn't been down this particular tunnel in a long time, and I'd forgotten what a difficult walk it was. The first lengthy stretch was not level — it was uphill, and pulling the cage with Yipes in it was backbreaking work. When I'd traveled here before, on my first trip outside the walls, I'd managed the entire walk in about twenty minutes. Tonight it would take hours, and even then I'd be stuck at the bottom of a tall ladder with no way to lift out the cage.

At the top of the ladder would be the wooden door that Yipes had once guided me through. It would be out in the open, but far enough from Bridewell that we wouldn't be seen as long as we reached it before light. From there we would need to travel carefully into the forest and find the place where the forest council was held, the place where Ander the bear made his home. He would be some help to me if only I could make it that far.

I wondered how Armon, Odessa, and Nicolas were faring, but mostly I thought of my father and hoped he and Pervis were safe in Bridewell. My great fear was that they were still within the walls looking for me, thinking I'd found myself in trouble and putting their lives in danger even as I'd already escaped with Yipes. Still, if they *had* gotten free of Bridewell, it was better that they weren't with me. There were many dangerous paths to come, and I had a terrible feeling that anyone traveling with me was putting his or her life in grave danger.

An hour passed, and then another. Yipes chattered on to keep me company as I stayed quiet, conserving my energy and focusing on the task of getting us at least as far as the ladder. I was spurred on by the thought of ogres tearing their way through the wall that held the secret door and chasing us down the tunnels until we were overtaken and returned to Grindall.

"I think we're getting close," said Murphy. He darted ahead in the dark, and I realized then that the lamp wasn't providing much light. Yipes saw me looking at it.

He shifted his weight in the cage and stared up at the lamp. “I turned it down as far as it would go to save fuel. It’s nearly out.” As if on cue, the light began to sputter and shrink even more. A moment later it went out entirely, and we were left in complete darkness.

“Is it just me, or does it seem as though things are getting more difficult all the time?” I asked.

“Just don’t get turned around and head in the wrong direction,” answered Yipes. “If you keep going straight ahead we should be to the end soon.”

Murphy scuttled up beside me and brushed my feet, startling me as he always did in the dark.

“Sorry about that,” he said. “I really must learn to let you know I’m coming.”

“How much farther?” I asked. I was so tired I wasn’t sure if I could pull the cage much more.

“It’s just up there a little, maybe five minutes if you really put your back into it,” Murphy replied.

Five more minutes of dragging the cage in the dirt sounded harder than climbing to the top of Mount Laythen, but I put the chain over my shoulder and started pulling again. Every muscle ached, and my hands stung with blisters from gripping the rough chain for so long. I stumbled into a wall and lost my grip on the chain, picked it up, and kept going in the dark. I felt as if I was sleepwalking, aimlessly trudging along in a nightmare that would never stop.

Thankfully, only a few minutes later my journey came to an end. I dropped the chain and felt the welcome rungs of the ladder and the cool earth of the walls around it. I sat down and rested, and it crossed my mind then that I could have taken the Jocasta out of its hiding place and used it for light.

I decided to pull it out and look at it, something I hadn't done in quite a while.

The moment it was out in the open air, the space we were in grew sharp with orange light. It was like a fire in my hand shooting flames on every wall. The light sped so far down the tunnel it scared me. It was as though the light were made of liquid and would travel like a wave all the way back into the library until Grindall saw it outlined against the secret door.

"That is quite the Jocasta," said Yipes. "Maybe you should keep it hidden in such a dark place."

I fumbled with the leather pouch and put the Jocasta back inside, but I left the top of the pouch open. The orange glow was contained, and I could point it wherever I chose in a way I'd never imagined. I pointed up the ladder to the door above and stood up.

"I'm going to leave you here and see if I can find help somewhere above," I said. "I hope I've grown enough since the last time I was here to lift that door and get out."

I was drained of so much energy that I had to stop every few rungs and rest, making sure my footing was solid as I went. When I finally reached the top, I took hold of the pouch around my neck and pulled. The leather string tightened around the Jocasta, and darkness returned.

"Okay, Alexa," I said out loud. "You can do this. One big push is all it will take."

Murphy had ridden up with me on my shoulder, and in the darkness I heard him leap from his perch and stand on the top rung of the ladder. I bent down my head and put my shoulder against the big door. Then I pushed with all my might.

It moved — only a little at first. But when I saw faint light creeping into the tunnel, I pushed even harder, until the opening was big enough for me to fit through. Murphy darted into the opening and hopped uncontrollably, yelling for me to keep pushing. I gave one last thrust, and the door jumped off my shoulder a few inches while I leaped for the opening.

I was hoping things wouldn't get any worse, but my strength wasn't enough to carry me all the way through to the outside. The door crashed back down and landed firmly on my back, pinning me between two worlds. I yelped but did not scream, the weight of the door not enough to really hurt me. I squirmed and tried to get free, but I had reached the end of my strength. My legs dangled behind me, and I laid my head on the cool earth, completely exhausted.

"How's it going up there?" It was Yipes yelling from somewhere far below in the tunnel. "I see a bit of light creeping in. Dawn is coming."

His words startled me back to life. I tried to look behind me and see the walls of Bridewell in the distance.

"Murphy, do you see the walls?" I asked.

"I do, and there are ogres at the towers. I don't think they can see this far, but I can't be sure. Stay still."

Murphy ran away into the nearby trees, and I lost sight of him. The best thing I could do was to remain still, so I put my head back down and hoped the light of day wouldn't come on too quickly. I moved my head as close to the opening in the door as I could and tried to talk to Yipes.

"I'm stuck, Yipes, and the sun is coming up. I don't know what to do."

"Oh," replied Yipes. "That's *very* unfortunate. Are you hurt?"

"No, not really, but I can't get free."

There was a long silence from below, and I wondered what Yipes was thinking. I heard rustling in the underbrush near a stand of trees outside, and a moment later Murphy was back . . . and he had someone else with him.

"It really is her! I can't believe it." It was a rabbit, one I'd met before.

"Malcolm, is that you?" I asked.

"Yes, ma'am. It's a pleasure to hear your voice." He hopped back and forth over my back and then came back around and sat in front of me. "*Hmmmm.* This *is* a problem, isn't it? We need someone bigger to help us."

"That's very smart of you, Malcolm. It's getting heavier on my back, and it's starting to really hurt. Can you find someone to help me?"

Malcolm seemed to stew on the thought

for a moment. He was a very clever rabbit, but I was worried he would take too long in figuring out a way to get me free.

Finally, his eyes brightened. "Yes! There *is* someone. It won't take but a moment to fetch him. Just wait here, and I'll come back."

Malcolm and Murphy darted off into the trees like two giddy dogs chasing a stick. "Hurry!" I called after them.

When they returned a few minutes later, the sun was coming up fast, and it was almost fully light outside. There were three of them now. Murphy was the smallest, then Malcolm. My face must have given away my despair at the sight of the third.

"Not big enough for you?" said Malcolm, an air of defeat in his voice. He had found Beaker the raccoon, who stood before me lolling from side to side, assessing the situation. The three of them put together were no match for the door, and it was starting to feel even heavier on my back.

"What's going on up there?" Yipes hollered from below. Malcolm and Beaker scattered into the underbrush until I told them it was only Yipes. This seemed to excite them even more as they talked among themselves about how to free me.

"This is hopeless," I said. I hung in the morning air, my breathing becoming harder and harder as the weight of the door worked against my back. I was getting weaker as the day was getting brighter, and I felt certain we were about to be discovered.

"How long were you planning to hang around up here?"

It was a voice from the ladder behind me, and it startled both me and the animals. Malcolm and Beaker were darting in every direction looking for cover — bumping into each other as they dashed from side to side — but Murphy just stood there and spoke a wonderful word that put a smile on my face.

"Pervis?"

"What?" I said, trying to swing my head around to where I could see.

"It's Pervis Kotcher!" cried Murphy.

"Are you hurt, Alexa?" It was indeed Pervis, standing below me on the ladder, pushing my feet and legs aside so that he could get right up close to the door that pinned me firmly on the ground.

"I am *so* glad to see you," I answered. "How did you find us?"

"Never mind about that. I need to know — are you hurt?"

"Only my pride," I answered. "Although

this door is quite heavy, and I can't get free of it."

Pervis sighed in relief, then took a moment to decide how he would proceed.

"You said you wouldn't leave the tunnels. See what happens when you disobey?"

There was a silence then, and I thought he was looking below, trying to figure out what we should do.

"But you did rescue Yipes, and I must say I find that completely unbelievable. How do you do these things, Alexa Daley?"

I stammered, trying to think what to say, but he didn't give me a chance to answer. Instead, he pushed ahead with a plan to get me free of the door.

"We're going to have to take a chance and make a run for the trees. I'll lift the door enough for you to get out, then you run with all your might for the grove. Don't look back until you're safely hidden away."

"What about you and Yipes?" I asked, not wanting to leave them behind in the tunnels.

"I don't have the tools we'll need to get Yipes out of the cage," he answered. "I'll have to lift him out and then carry him to safety."

Pervis paused for a moment as Malcolm

and Beaker came bouncing back to the door and skittered around nervously.

"Do you have your spyglass, Alexa?" asked Pervis.

I nodded.

"When you get to the stand of trees, use it to survey the walls of Bridewell. I'll bring up Yipes and hold him here until I see Malcolm come darting out into the open. That will be the signal."

"All right — but you'll need to run as fast as you can with that cage. I don't think you'll have much time to reach the grove."

Pervis nodded and started down the ladder.

"Pervis?" I said.

He stopped and looked up at me. "What?"

"Where's my father?"

It was a question I had been afraid to ask.

"I don't know, Alexa. We split up after we entered Bridewell. He was going for the smoking room and I went around the courtyard. When I heard all the ruckus in the library, I just knew you'd used that secret door. I thought maybe I'd find you down here."

He sighed deeply and touched me on the leg.

"He can take care of himself, Alexa. Right now we have to get you and Yipes out of here."

"Before we go on you have to promise me something," I said.

"What's that?"

"You have to go back and find him."

Pervis seemed to mull over my request before answering.

"All right, I'll do it. As long as I have you safe in the trees and away from Grindall and the ogres, I'll go back for him."

I felt relieved — not only would he go back and find my father, but he would be safe from traveling the dangerous road that lay ahead of me. Pervis inched up a little farther on the ladder and put his shoulder into the door.

"Malcolm — can you see the guard tower?" I asked.

"Oh, yes, indeed I can. I eat many carrots. Carrots are good for eyesight, you know? I can see quite a long ways on a clea—"

"Malcolm! Just tell me if it's clear to go or not," I said.

"Oh, sorry, I didn't mean to get carried away." He peered out along the walls of Bridewell for a long moment, then turned back to me.

"It's clear!" he shouted.

I relayed the message to Pervis, and he wasted no time in pushing up the door enough to let me out. It felt wonderful to have the weight off my back. I quickly darted free, then ran for the trees as fast and as low as I could. Malcolm, Beaker, and Murphy zigzagged in front of me, moving from clump to clump in the underbrush.

When we arrived in the grove of trees, I crouched low and took out my spyglass, aiming it at the walls of Bridewell. There on the closest tower stood an ogre, staring out into the Dark Hills. As I watched, another ogre arrived at the tower and looked toward the grove of trees. I stayed very still until the two ogres began to talk. Then I looked back at the trapdoor I'd been freed of.

Pervis had yet to arrive, so I waited, whispering in the trees.

"Have you seen anyone else out here?" I asked Malcolm and Beaker.

"No," Beaker reported. "But Ander has been keeping us busy on the watch. We all smelled something rotten when those creatures took over Bridewell. And it was very strange how Bridewell emptied out. We keep a close eye on the walled city. It seems to be a place where a great many important things take place."

There was a nervous pause from the animals, and then Malcolm added something more.

"Things aren't as they used to be in the forest, Alexa. Things are . . . well, they're different. You'll see."

I asked him what he meant, but he wouldn't tell me anything else. My thoughts drifted to Armon, my father, Warvold, Nicolas — everything was coming unraveled. It seemed so many of the people I loved were in grave danger, and I wondered how things could ever be put back together again.

The door tipped open slightly, and I knew that Pervis had arrived with Yipes at the top of the ladder. Peering through my spyglass I saw with some relief that the two ogres were arguing, pointing into the Dark Hills and pushing at each other.

"Go, Malcolm! Now!"

Malcolm was momentarily stunned and darted around in circles in the trees. Then he found his bearings and hopped quickly toward the door where Pervis and Yipes lay hidden.

The door flew open, and the cage was set outside in the open. Then Pervis emerged, and the door disappeared from sight, back into its resting place on the ground. Pervis took hold of the cage and started running across the open toward the trees with Malcolm leading the way. It was a mighty task for a small man like Pervis, but he managed to run quite fast with his arms wrapped around the cage.

I looked into my spyglass again and watched as the ogres continued to look out into the Dark Hills. One of them turned toward the courtyard, and the other crept down the side of the tower back into Bridewell. The remaining ogre turned then, looked directly at me, then scanned the forest to my right.

When I pulled the spyglass down to see where Pervis and Yipes were, I couldn't find them.

"Where are they?" I asked.

"Down here!" answered Murphy. He was scampering down the line of trees to where Pervis had hidden in the low bushes.

"Good work, Alexa," said Pervis. We were all safe in the grove, and we carefully moved farther back into the trees, where we sat in a circle.

"It feels so good to sit down and rest," I said, fully exhausted.

"I can't tell you how much I would like

to stand up," said Yipes. "They only let me out of here to go to the bathroom, and I haven't done that in quite a while."

I smiled as Pervis took the cage off into the trees where the two of them would figure out some way for Yipes to relieve himself.

In the morning light, I remembered how much I loved the sound of wind through the trees. I laid back and closed my eyes, and I was comforted by the sound of a million tiny leaves dancing on a summer morning.

As the world spun out of control all around me, I drifted into a deep sleep and dreamed of animals and giants. And I heard the voice of Elyon through the wind.

I am sorry, Alexa. Your father's time has come. He will leave the land of the living before the sun rises twice more.

I woke with a scream and found that things were not as I'd left them.

PART 2

CHAPTER 13

THE LESSON IN THE LEAF

Yipes was sitting in the cage, which was next to me, rubbing his head with one hand. When I'd awoken, it had frightened him into leaping up and banging his little head. It took me a moment to shake away the sleepiness and remember where I was.

"That must have been some dream," said Yipes. "I'm not sure I want to hear about it."

"Where has everyone gone?" I asked, startled to find only Yipes there in the grove with me. It was warmer now, but there was a lot of shade thrown from the trees above, and I couldn't be sure how long I'd slept or if I'd slept at all.

"Pervis didn't want to wake you. He's gone to find your father."

"What about the rest?"

"I don't know," said Yipes. "The animals have all scattered — including Murphy — which seems a bit strange. I think they're watching for Grindall, but I can't understand them so I'm not sure. They're around here somewhere."

I stood in the grove of trees and took the Jocasta's leather bag in my hand. I wanted to remove it and bury it deep in the ground so I wouldn't have to listen to it.

"I don't want this terrible Jocasta anymore!" I yelled. "I'm hearing things I don't want to hear, things I hope are not true."

Yipes took his hand away from his head and folded his hands together, rubbing his thumbs back and forth in his lap. He was sitting cross-legged, but it was such a small cage that he still had to turn his head down to fit inside. I stood up and turned away from him. Through the trees and way off in the distance, I could see the walls of Bridewell, cold and alone, empty but for Grindall and his ogres — and maybe my own father, alone and searching for me in vain.

"I used to love Bridewell," I said, the late-morning breeze lifting my hair in little waves. "When my father and I would go there — when I was younger — there was nothing I loved more than the excitement and the mystery of my summers. To explore Renny Lodge and walk down all the cobbled streets pretending I was on special assignment from Warvold himself — some secret task he'd asked me to do — those times were the heartbeat of my childhood. I would imagine that Pervis or Grayson or Ganesh were spies and I'd been sent to uncover them. But there was something special about those times, because while I enjoyed my fun, there was no *real* danger." I paused, frightened by my own words. Somehow saying them made me even more aware that those carefree days were gone, replaced by something almost *too* real, *too* dangerous.

A wayward leaf fell from a tree far above, dangled on the air, then landed at my feet. I picked it up.

"It's summertime, Yipes. Leaves shouldn't fall in summertime. This one's gone old before its time."

I took the leaf over to the cage that held Yipes and poked the stem through so that it stood like a flower.

"Bridewell is taken, and The Land of Elyon is failing," I said. "I feel so lost, Yipes. I want to go home and find things as they used to be. I want to visit Bridewell and explore within the safety of its walls for as long as I please. I want this adventure to be over."

The wind turned up and blew the leaf back and forth against the cage, but it didn't escape the trap I'd put it in.

"You're growing up, Alexa, and I'm afraid there's no turning back the clock," Yipes told me gently. "I remember when I was a boy, all I wanted to do was grow up and get away into the wild. But there came a time when I wished I could be a boy again, that I could turn the world back into a simple place."

He took the stem of the leaf between his finger and thumb and twirled it, looking at it in a way I didn't understand.

"We can't go back, Alexa," he said. "We can't go back once we've started growing up, and the world can't be made simple again."

Yipes let the leaf go, pushing it through a hole in the cage. The wind came up and carried it across the grove, where it skidded on the ground and bounced on the breeze out of sight.

"There is something we *can* do," Yipes continued. "We can reclaim this place for good — we can restore it to what it once was. And then maybe the places of your past will feel something like they used to."

Yipes was right. I knew I couldn't go back, and I knew it was entirely up to me to defeat the terrible evil that had entered our world. But why did my father have to die as part of Elyon's plan? I tried to put the idea out of my mind, but it wouldn't go away.

"A single leaf, fallen before its time," said Yipes. "I wonder what can be learned from a leaf like that, one that will be brown and dead in a day or a week as all its friends stay green and true in the trees above."

"I don't see a lesson there, Yipes. I only see the two of us, lost and alone, with a task beyond our ability before us."

Yipes stared off in the direction where the leaf had blown away. He thought for a moment, then kept on with his prodding.

"You're not looking hard enough."

I thought more of the leaf that had danced away to its death, where it would crumble and decay into the earth, no one to care about it or notice it had gone. I was too tired to think, and all I really wanted to do was go home and sleep for days and days.

"Here's what I think," Yipes said, aware from the look on my face that I was unlikely to offer much in the way of an answer. "That thing, that tiny part of The Land of Elyon, is gone but not entirely forgotten. Elyon had his reason for making it fall into our lap, just as he had his reason for sending you and me on this journey. Sometimes we see something as plain as a dying leaf and our hearts grow sad, but we must always hold true and fight on, Alexa. Whatever happens to us, we will not be forgotten in the end. He *will* remember us."

I couldn't bring myself to tell him what I'd heard just moments ago, that my father wouldn't live much longer, that he would join the leaf before too long. And yet Yipes's words did comfort me a little. Even if this adventure were to take my life and that of my father, we would not be forgotten or left behind. Somehow I began to think better of the leaf. Maybe in death it would find something more than we could imagine.

"What shall we do?" I asked Yipes, thinking I'd had enough of mulling over the questions of this life and the next. "I can't leave you here by yourself, but we really must be getting on. Where on earth has Murphy gone off to?"

"I think we'll have to wait here," Yipes told me, "at least until Murphy shows up again. You look like you haven't slept in days, and this is the safest place I can think of to take some time to regain your strength. That little nap you took won't be enough to get you all the way to the Tenth City."

I protested and argued for a while, but I *was* awfully tired. Sitting there in the grove as the noonday sun hovered overhead, I began to feel sleepy.

"I'll just lie here for a moment," I said, and I reclined right next to the cage, my head resting on my pack. We talked some more in the soft heat of the day. The sound of Yipes's words and the trees swaying overhead began to garble together until I could no longer stay awake. And then I fell into a long, deep sleep.

"Alexa — wake up."

I lurched forward and groaned awake, my body surprisingly sore from the hard ground beneath me. It was still light out, but there was now a coolness in the air around me.

"Now *that* was a nap," said Yipes, smiling from inside his little cage.

I rubbed my eyes and yawned, wondering how much of the day I'd slept away.

"Is it almost evening?" I asked.

"Not quite. It's morning, Alexa. I kept thinking you would wake up, but it remained warm last night and you kept right on sleeping."

"What?" I exclaimed. "I can't have slept all day and night, can I?"

Yipes grinned at me, and I realized I really *had* slept that long. I must have been even more exhausted than I'd thought.

"Yipes, we have to be moving along," I said, gathering my pack and making ready to go. "I know it's just the two of us, but we can't waste any more time here in the trees. I'll have to drag you along until we find our way to the forest council."

"Are you sure there are only the two of us?" asked Yipes.

"What do you mean? Where's Murphy?"

Yipes put his finger to his lips and became very still. Then he whispered, *"Listen."*

All I could hear was the rustling of the leaves in the trees. But Yipes had grown up in these mountains. He could keenly sense people and animals approaching. The first discernable sound that I heard, besides the wind in the trees, was very clear — a shrill, loud noise in the distance. I looked up.

"Squire!" I said. We hadn't seen her in a long while, and I welcomed her presence.

She circled high in the air but did not descend, which got me to wondering what she might be seeing from the sky. How I wished I could see with her eyes and know all the secrets of The Land of Elyon so easily.

"Why doesn't she come down to us?" I asked. "I think she would find it quite interesting to see you behind those little bars."

Yipes was listening carefully, his head turned to one side.

"She's here to warn us," he said. "Danger is near."

This was not what I was hoping to hear. Caught alone and defenseless with a very small man trapped in a cage was about as helpless a situation as I could imagine.

"I can't leave you again, Yipes," I said. I looked all around for a place to hide the cage, but the best I could do was drag it between two trees that grew together at the bottom and branched out. We huddled in the grass as I peered through the V at the center of the two trees, keeping my head low so I wouldn't be seen.

We waited and listened until finally I began to hear something new in the distance — something large. Whatever it was, it was moving slowly, lumbering along, breaking twigs underfoot as it went. Could it be an ogre? Or maybe it was Ander, the giant grizzly bear, come to free Yipes from his cage. As I stared out into the grove of trees, I saw something unexpected. It was Murphy, scampering to and fro, yelping at the top of his lungs over the lumbering sound coming from somewhere behind him.

"Alexa? Yipes?" he called. "Where have you gone? Come out if you can hear me!" Malcolm came bounding up behind Murphy, and the two of them circled and sniffed where we had been.

I whispered as loudly as I could, "*Murphy* — we're over here. Where have you been?"

Murphy and Malcolm hopped and darted in our direction. Then Murphy came up the tree to the V where I looked out and sat right in front of my face.

"Oh, I do love surprises, don't you?" he said.

The heavy sound of something approaching grew closer, louder. I thought I saw something in the trees moving toward us.

"Only a moment more," said Murphy, "and I do believe you'll both be very surprised."

I was just about to scold Murphy for leaving us to wonder what might be coming . . . but just at that moment Armon came into view, his giant shoulders so high up in the air, his arms pushing away limbs of trees as though they were toothpicks. I was overjoyed at the sight of him.

"Armon!" I ran from behind the trees into the open space of the grove and stood before him, but instead of embracing me he moved aside, and I saw an even greater surprise. Behind him was Warvold, looking very excited to see me.

I ran to Warvold and threw myself into him. Armon put his giant hand atop my head and scattered my hair from side to side. I couldn't imagine how, but we'd found our way back to one another.

When I looked over my shoulder from my embrace with Warvold, I saw that Armon had gone to the trees I'd hidden behind. He peered into the V, put his whole arm in between, and pulled out the cage with Yipes trapped inside. He then took two giant strides into the grove and set down the cage between us where we all stood staring. Warvold knelt down next to the cage and peered inside.

"I thought I'd never see you again," he

said to Yipes. "It looks as though you've gotten yourself into quite a bit of trouble in my absence."

The two of them looked at each other with great joy, old friends finally back together again.

"We might be wise to leave him in the cage," said Armon. "He's easier to look after this way."

Yipes only smiled, overcome with happiness at this reunion.

"Then again, he can be quite useful at times. I suppose we ought to let him out," said Armon.

He reached down and put his fingers into some of the holes in the cage. Then, with no effort at all, he pulled his hands apart and the cage split open like an old burlap sack. Out hopped Yipes.

He kept on with his hopping as he went around our circle, touching a sleeve or receiving an embrace. Then the reason for his strange behavior became apparent as he darted off into the woods looking for a place he could call a bathroom.

"I don't understand, Warvold," I said. "How did you find us?"

Warvold started the story and then had to begin again when Yipes returned (looking very relieved, I might add). It would seem that Armon had thought the *Warwick Beacon* might make it back around to Lathbury while we were busy rescuing Yipes. And so, after eluding the black swarm, he had spent the night hours running to the cliffs, right to the same place where we had left Renny. Down the rope he'd gone, through the mist, looking out along the water for the *Warwick Beacon* all that next day and night. Finally, a few hours ago, the ship had shown itself on the horizon, the winds having carried it around the far side of The Land of Elyon while I slept. The only stop the ship had made was at Castalia, where Balmoral had gone back to his people.

"It was hard to let him stay, but they need him there, and we couldn't risk losing him in the coming days," Warvold explained. "Castalia must be rebuilt, and Balmoral must lead them. He is where he ought to be, just like the rest of us."

Finishing the story, Warvold told of riding on the back of a giant through the haze of morning, how Armon was tireless in his effort to make it to the forest council, and what a wonderful adventure it had been.

"He is a most amazing creature," said Warvold, looking at Armon with great pleasure. “We came upon you here as we made our way. As we come near to the end, we are back together again, as it should be.”

Yipes was free. Armon and Warvold were with me and Murphy once more. I felt a sudden wave of confidence that we could yet succeed in our task. And then I noticed Murphy looking around the many faces, confused.

“Where is Odessa?” he asked.

CHAPTER 14

FENWICK FOREST

I assured everyone that the most promising place to meet up with Odessa again would be at the forest council. It was here that I had first encountered Odessa with her son, Sherwin, and it was here that we hoped to find help in our quest across the forest and toward the Tenth City.

At the behest of Armon and Warvold, we drew deeper into the wild, away from Bridewell. As we neared the road that led between Turlock and Bridewell, we began finding the stones that used to make up the wall alongside it. Big square blocks sat surrounded by weeds and underbrush. It was a sea of broken wall, scattered through the trees and growing old as though those stones had been there all along. I had a sudden longing to turn and run toward my home in Lathbury, to lie on the bed in the privacy of my own room and sleep the day away alone.

"This road is watched," Warvold warned us. "We must be very careful as we cross into Fenwick Forest. It's hard to say what awaits us in the dark of the wood."

We sent Murphy and Malcolm ahead to scout while the rest of us waited and whispered among the stones and the trees.

I whispered to Armon, "I'm so happy you're safe. How on earth did you escape the bats?"

He smiled and leaned down close to me. "A giant is faster of foot than you might imagine," he said. "And I have a few hiding places of my own for times such as these."

The sun rose in the sky, bringing the heat of late morning with it. It frightened me to think of the day drifting away, taking my father with it. I turned back in the direction of Bridewell and saw Warvold crouching in the dirt, looking at me as if he knew I was concerned about something.

"What troubles you, Alexa?"

"Things keep getting more dangerous," I answered. "I fear something terrible will happen soon, and it scares me to think about it."

Warvold nodded, his eyes glazed over as if he were lost in a distant memory.

"I have felt the same as you," he told me.

"When we left Balmoral in Castalia, I voiced my fears to him, wondering what he might say. He told me that when you've lived through a generation of troubled times, slaving for an evil man as he has, watching your friends and family fall before you —" Warvold stopped short, overcome with anger and sadness. "When you've lived through a thing like that," he continued, "nothing seems dangerous anymore. It all just seems normal, as though every day brings hardship, and to think it might be otherwise is the way of fools."

"It seems like a dark way to live, never expecting to see the world rid of things like Grindall and the ogres," I said.

Warvold smiled at me, his anger with the past softening. "Balmoral told me one more thing before he disappeared into the mist at Castalia. He told me the world is full of danger and full of stories. And then he asked me what sort of story we would have to tell if there were nothing for good people to fight for."

Warvold touched my shoulder and looked deep into my eyes. "I think we were meant to fight a good fight, and I think we're better for fighting it."

I hadn't thought of things in quite that way before, but I supposed Balmoral and

Warvold were right. If my father had to die in order to free The Land of Elyon from the evils of Abaddon, at least he would die trying to preserve Bridewell and its people. His story would be a good one, remembered and talked about.

"We can cross now." It was Murphy, back from checking the road. He was fidgeting on top of the rock I was hiding behind. As I stood to go, he leaped onto my pack and held on to the leather with his tiny claws.

"Oh, no, you don't," said Warvold. "We need you to stay out front and watch for anything unusual. A rustle in the bushes, a strange smell — if you sense the slightest oddity, you must warn us."

Murphy jumped down immediately and darted back to the road, crossed over, and disappeared into the trees on the other side.

"Off we go then," said Warvold. "Across the road and quickly!"

Armon went first and was across the road in three giant steps before the rest of us could get started. Warvold followed, then Yipes, and finally me. We ran across the road as quickly as we could, down into the thick woods on the other side, Armon clearing a path before us as we went. There was no sign of Squire, gone off again to places I couldn't see.

Something was different about the forest from the way I'd remembered it. Before, when I'd come to visit the forest council, it had seemed wild and untamed but still somehow friendly and inviting. Today I felt afraid of the forest. It was darker than I remembered it, more forbidding. Had something changed this place in my short absence?

"Slow down, Armon," Yipes called. "You'll get us lost."

Armon stopped and looked back, waiting for the group to arrive at his feet. It didn't matter how many times I stood at the foot of this giant — each time I was newly amazed at his grandeur, his overwhelming presence. As I stood beneath him and craned my neck to see his face, my fear of Fenwick Forest began to fade.

"There used to be a trail near here," said Yipes. "It seems that things have grown over. This place is different, wilder than when I last passed through."

Warvold nodded his agreement and whispered, *"Abaddon."*

"What do you mean?" asked Armon.

Warvold looked around in all directions and squinted up into the trees. He continued, “A long time ago, I traveled through the Sly Field and into Fenwick Forest with a friend of mine. He was a great explorer in his own right, and though we did not find the Tenth City on that day, we both agreed that something else was near these parts. Wherever it is that Abaddon makes his home, it’s not too terribly far from the woods.”

“Yes, but why the sudden change in the way this place feels, the way it grows wilder?” asked Yipes.

“Abaddon is mustering all his powers to find us,” Warvold explained. “I think he knew we would come this way, and so he has made our journey more treacherous. I fear things will change for the worse as we travel deeper into the woods.”

The hair rose on my neck, and a cold chill ran through my body.

“Who was the friend, the one who traveled with you?” I asked, though I felt sure I knew the answer before he offered it.

“His name was Cabeza de Vaca — a very interesting man, well traveled and always in search of the Tenth City. He presides over the Western Kingdom now, though I haven’t seen him in ages.”

Cabeza de Vaca. I’d read his book, used it to judge the distance to the bottom of the tunnel on my first journey outside the walls. It was comforting to hear his name once more.

"In any case, we must travel carefully," said Warvold. "This place is not what it once was, and neither are the creatures that make their home here."

"I think I can find my way to the forest council," said Yipes. "But I wonder now if we ought to go there."

It was a terrible thought. Could it be that Abaddon had somehow turned the forest animals against us? If so, I surely wouldn't want to stand face-to-face with Ander. Even Armon would have a battle on his hands trying to contain a creature so fierce.

"I think we risk it," said Armon. "Abaddon may have turned this wood into a dark place, but we have to hope the animals will be able to help us find our way."

There was silence among the group, as we listened to the wind sweep in around us. Some of the largest of the trees groaned as if the wind might tear them from their roots.

"Yipes, you jump up there on Armon's shoulders," said Warvold. "The two of you can lead the way."

We continued deeper into the forest and

found that the farther we went, the more the trees groaned against the pushing of the wind. The trunks became darker, limbs fallen, and our passage was hindered by thorny walls of dead blackberry bushes and thick brown vines along the floor of the wood.

"Warvold," I said, taken aback by what I was seeing, "this place is dying."

He kept walking without answering me, and I felt his sadness at the sight of this once-great forest. A gust of wind blew from somewhere far away, and in the distance we heard a mighty cracking of wood and the sound of a tree falling to the ground. The trees were growing old before our eyes, and looking up I realized that there were no leaves left on them, no leaves flying through the air on the wind. It was summer in The Land of Elyon, but I saw now that the deeper we went into the forest, the more it seemed as if winter had somehow come to this place — a winter without the blistering cold, but a winter nonetheless. Everything was dormant or dead.

"We're close," said Yipes, turning toward us from his perch on Armon's shoulders. "Only a little farther and we'll be in the grove."

It was impossible to keep quiet now. With every step Armon took, the forest floor cracked with dead branches. If someone was waiting for us in the grove he would be well aware of our arrival. Armon fought through a final thick casing of thorny bushes with his sword, and there before us was the secret place where I'd first met the forest council.

The lush grass and towering trees of green and gold were no longer part of this place. All that remained were the stones the animals had sat upon, surrounded by a sea of death — fallen trees crusted with wrinkled leaves, the lush grass turned to brown stubble. At the far end of the grove sat a large, lonely figure, his head turned down to the ground. It was the only animal, and as we emerged out of the trees and into the open the beast lifted his head and looked at us.

"I had a feeling you might find your way back here." It was Ander, the grizzly bear and keeper of the forest, and he didn't look at all happy to see us.

Other animals crept into view and sat among the fallen trees and ancient stones. Darius and Sherwin were not among them, and many of the faces were not familiar or friendly. As we stood in the gloom of the grove, Ander said something I hadn't expected him to say.

"Why have you done this to my forest?" There was anger in his eyes as he rose to his full height and glared in our direction. He began to shake with rage as he looked around the grove. "Answer me!"

I was the only one who understood this booming request. Everyone else heard a monstrous roar of the kind they'd never heard before. I had hoped the forest council would be a place where we could find help from friends. Instead I felt more afraid and unsure than ever.

"What's he saying, Alexa?" Warvold asked. I didn't have a chance to answer him, for at that very moment Ander began charging toward us.

I held my breath and hoped something would stop Ander from his attack. If he wasn't stopped, he would meet with Armon first and the two of them would tear each other to shreds. How could he think that we had done this to his home? Everything seemed to be moving in slow motion as Armon steadied himself, and Ander advanced quickly from the far side of the grove. For the first time that I could remember, I put a direct question to Elyon, hoping for an answer that could stop the charging grizzly bear.

What shall I do, Elyon?

To my surprise, the answer came the moment I'd thought of the question.

Stand between Ander and Armon.

Without further thought, I ran in front of Armon and stood between him and the approaching bear, certain that my short life was about to come to a painful and quick end.

CHAPTER 15

THE GROVE

I remember hearing Warvold's voice, screaming for me to get out of the way. But I stood frozen as Ander came within a few feet of my face, his teeth gleaming in the sun that swept through the branches of the bare trees. I looked into his eyes and he looked into mine, and that final moment seemed to last a lifetime. In his eyes I saw such terrible sadness, a misery he alone could understand as his world was dying all around him. I tried to send a message back in my own eyes: *We didn't do this. We need your help to put it back the way it was.*

Ander came so close and with such force that nothing else existed. Not the wood or my friends or my world — only those desperate, sad eyes. Later I would learn that grizzly bears will often charge an intruder, only to turn at the last second and run off into the trees, as if it were a game to see if the intruder would turn and try to run away. I could not imagine Ander any closer than he was when he turned, his massive shoulder grazing mine as he went by. After he was past me, he stopped faster than I thought possible and reared up on his two back legs, his back to Armon and the rest of us.

Ander made a sound then that I will never forget. It was a sound of anguish and despair, a haunting growl that was caught on the wind and carried through the forest. He was crying.

I sat down in the dead grass of the grove and watched as Ander came back down on his four legs, turned, and stood before us. The many animals who had gathered in the grove were moving closer, acting as though they would all attack us together at any moment. Badgers and mountain lions and wolves — too much for us to overcome.

"Leave them be," Ander said to the animals. "We must take a moment to talk this through before proceeding."

The forest had taken us captive, and there would be no escaping from all the animals of the wood. If they wanted to tear us apart, then we would be torn apart. As Ander retreated to the center of the grove and sat down, I knew we would have to convince him that we were not responsible for what had happened to his home. Either that or we would never see the light of another day.

"Your foolishness may well have saved us," said Warvold. I looked up at him and saw a look of great relief in his eyes. "You will have to talk with him, Alexa. No one else can understand what he's saying."

I started walking slowly toward the center of the grove where the mighty bear sat all alone. Armon came up beside me, sword drawn, and kept my slow pace.

"You'd better stay back with the others, Armon," I cautioned. "He won't trust me if you're towering over us, waiting to do him in."

Armon bent down on one knee and put his hand on my shoulder.

"Are you sure about this?" he asked.

"No, I'm really not sure at all. But I know this bear. Unless Abaddon has somehow possessed him as he has the forest, I think I can talk to him."

Armon sighed deeply, stood, and returned his sword to its sheath. I walked the rest of the way by myself. The crunching of the broken forest lay beneath me as I went, and the air was dirty like the road to

Bridewell on a dry day.

Sitting down in front of Ander I felt a terrible loss as I looked at his old claws clumped with dirt. He was an old bear, full of memory, of things I'd only dreamed.

"I'm so sorry, Ander," I began. "But we didn't do this to your forest. It was someone else."

"Was it, Alexa?"

"Yes, it was. Maybe we can put it back the way it was if you'll help us find our way."

Ander put his head down near mine and sniffed the air around me, blowing my hair back as he exhaled. Tiny droplets of water sprayed from his nose and landed on my cheeks. I wiped them away.

"You tried to help us once," he said. "When men built the walls that separated everything, you tried to help us."

I nodded, not knowing what to say.

"But it was men who built the walls to begin with, men who thought nothing of us in all their planning and destroying."

Ander looked across the grove at Warvold, and I turned to see how my friend would react. Warvold couldn't know what Ander was saying, and he was not looking in our direction. Instead, he was standing next to a fallen tree, running his fingers over a broken branch. It looked as though he was feeling very sorry for himself.

"Why must you always make such trouble?" Ander asked.

"I'm only a child," I said, not knowing what else I could offer. "I don't know what to say to you, only that we're sorry the forest is failing and that we want to make it better."

"I wonder how long it would have taken for you to come and cut down all the trees for your houses and your buildings," said Ander. "This forest has been taken by a terrible evil, but in years to come I fear you'd have taken it from us out of your own greed."

"No, Ander! We would never do that," I said. "You have to believe me."

Ander looked at me and for the first time there was kindness in his eyes.

"I do believe you, Alexa Daley. There are some of your kind who want what's best for everything that lives in The Land of Elyon. There are others who want to destroy it." He looked again at Warvold. "Even he wanted only to protect, not to destroy, though he harmed us in the process."

We sat alone in the grove for a long, silent moment.

"What is it that you want from me, Alexa? I fear my time is coming to an end along with the woods."

There was nothing more to do but boldly ask for what we needed.

"Can you help us find the Tenth City, Ander? I don't know what we'll do when we get there, but maybe it will help restore this place if we can find it."

Ander was quiet. He sat thinking, stewing on the problem, trying to decide if a young girl could be trusted with such an immense responsibility.

"What is that you have there around your neck?" he asked me.

I clutched the stone in the small leather pouch before speaking.

"It's the last Jocasta," I answered.

Ander's eyes widened and he moved his head down near mine once more.

"I knew you had a Jocasta but not . . . the last. Let me have a look at it."

I hesitated, then undid the leather pouch and removed the stone, holding it out in front of me. It lit up the grove with orange and gold, and for a moment the place seemed to come alive again.

Ander sighed and looked all around him, remembering what it had once been like.

"I have a secret to tell you, Alexa. One

that might help you find what you're looking for."

I put the Jocasta back inside the pouch and waited for Ander to tell me the secret.

"There are things a few of us animals know that elude human understanding. We're born with certain . . . knowledge — knowledge that is only useful at a time such as this." He paused a moment and I listened as a hush came over the grove and all the animals seemed to lean in around us.

"The stone will show you the way," he said. "When you reach the mist of the Sly Field, hold the stone out in front of you. Where others have failed in the Sly Field, you will succeed. Follow where it leads you, and you may yet find the Tenth City."

We both smiled.

"If I find it, if I can defeat Abaddon, I'll do everything I can to restore this place," I said.

"I know you will, Alexa."

Murphy came out of the grove and landed on my knee, looking at me with concern.

"Someone is coming, Alexa. The animals are stirring."

I listened along with Ander and heard the faint sound of something approaching from the woods. A moment later, Odessa came into the clearing. I was happy to see her.

"Odessa!" I said.

Ander sniffed at the air, his big head bouncing back and forth as he stretched his nose out from side to side. As I watched Odessa slowly approach us, I glanced around the grove and noticed something peculiar. All the animals had gone away, leaving bare stones strewn with dirt and leaves. Only Ander remained.

"There is something foul in the air," said Ander. I smelled it as well, the terrible odor of rotting flesh.

Odessa crept forward a few more steps, and then I heard the sound of beings crashing through the trees from every direction, moving fast. I could see their heads bobbing through the trees, their swollen shoulders knocking down limbs as they came, the black cloaks, and the hideous faces.

The ogres were upon us, closing in from all sides.

"Odessa, how could you?" said Ander. He was astounded at the sight of these creatures, and we both knew without hesitation that Odessa had led them to this sacred place, although my understanding might have been deeper than his. I looked back at my companions and saw that they, too, were dumbstruck by this turn of events.

There was nothing we could do as Grindall came into the clearing with a dreadful grin on his face, his menacing laugh echoing through the grove and chilling the air around us.

CHAPTER 16

CAPTURED

The ogres stood all around the grove, their breathing labored and soggy. I stayed where I was, afraid that even the slightest movement might cause one of the ogres to turn angry. They were wild, unpredictable creatures. Everything about them made me nervous and afraid. Only Grindall could control them, his voice like a hypnotic spell from which the ogres could not escape.

Ander backed away from me, moving toward one of the ogres, then turned and ran out of the grove. The ogres did not move. They were focused entirely on keeping me and my companions trapped.

Armon drew his sword, the sound of metal on metal ringing through the trees. He looked fierce enough to take on all of the ten ogres circling the grove, but a few seconds after the sword was drawn everything changed. One of the ogres took hold of Warvold, another Yipes, and a third had his hand on my back, lifting me in the air before I could turn and see him coming.

"Armon the giant." It was Grindall, his slippery voice bringing the ogres to a quick silence. "After all our searching we come upon you unprotected in this rotted forest. How convenient for me."

He looked around the open space and saw that he had three of his foes trapped, with seven more ogres surrounding Armon. The ogre who'd picked me up knelt down and set me in front of him, but his huge hand remained tightly gripped around my waist. I felt the material on my tunic turning slimy, cold, and slick against my skin. His hand was like a thick, wet mop tied tightly around my waist.

"It appears as though I have gained the upper hand," Grindall gloated. "All of my most hated enemies together in one place, taken unaware by our approach. I would have hoped for a little more of a challenge."

I could tell that Armon was having a difficult time putting down the sword. He wanted desperately to protect his friends, and yet he knew that with one quick squeeze of the ogres' hands three of us would be finished.

"Armon," I said, "put down the sword.

There's nothing you can do now. There's nothing any of us can do."

He hesitated, looking all around him, then heaved a great sigh and tossed the sword into the middle of the grove at Grindall's feet. Grindall threw back his head and laughed wickedly. He bent down and tried to pick up the weapon, but it was so big he could barely get it off the ground. Irritated, he called to one of the ogres, "Pick this up, you fool! Get it out of my way."

An ogre took the sword and flung it into the woods. It clanged to a stop beneath a moss-covered tree stump.

"Now then, where were we?" Grindall was enjoying himself far too much. "Oh, yes, I remember — I was about to have Warvold brought to me so that I might have a word with him."

The ogre that had hold of Warvold quickly stepped toward Grindall. With strong arms he pushed Warvold to his knees and stood breathing heavily a few feet away.

"Get back, you beast!" said Grindall. "I can hardly stand the smell of you so close."

The ogre backed up farther and took his guard with the others encircling Armon.

"Bring me the others," Grindall commanded. "I want them all at my feet while I give them as much regrettable news as I can think of."

The wet hand tightened around my waist and hoisted me into the air. I was dropped on my knees next to Warvold as Yipes was marched over and pushed to the ground with the two of us. I saw Murphy sitting on a stump to my left, free for the moment, and I hoped he wouldn't try anything foolish and get himself in trouble like the rest of us.

"Don't worry, Alexa." It was Warvold, whispering to me.

"Oh, on the contrary, *do* worry, Alexa!" roared Grindall. "You've failed . . . as I knew you would. I have captured everyone with the power to stop me — Warvold and Yipes — and the two most precious of all — Alexa Daley and Armon the giant. In all the far reaches of the land, you four are the greatest enemies of Abaddon. How pleased he must be with me."

He stifled a laugh and looked at Armon, surrounded by ogres. Then he returned his gaze to the four of us at his feet. Odessa strode up next to him and sat down. Grindall ran his long fingers over her coat.

"Wolves. They simply cannot be trusted," he said. "Unless of course you're me. Then they can be very useful."

Grindall stared at Warvold with a peculiar smile on his face.

"Look what's become of your beloved Land of Elyon. Thistles and thorns covering a dead forest. It would seem the powers that rule are not the ones you claim."

"Get on with it, Victor. What do you aim to do with us? Where will you take us?" asked Warvold.

"More to the point, where will *you* take *me?*" answered Grindall. He looked at the leather bag hanging around my neck.

"It will only help us find what you seek if you leave it around my neck," I said, sure of what he was thinking. Victor Grindall had searched for the last Jocasta for a very long time, and now he wanted only to possess it.

"I see," said Grindall. He took the leather pouch in his hand and toyed with it. "All the same, I would feel so much better if I could keep it myself."

He pulled up on the pouch and yanked the leather necklace over my head, releasing the Jocasta from my control. Then he opened the pouch and pulled out the stone, which shone brightly in his hand. There was a collective gasp in the grove from the ogres as they looked at the treasure before them. They seemed afraid of it, as though it might destroy them if they were to touch it.

I had finally lost control of the last Jocasta. I felt sure that the quest had also been lost, that I was near the end of my journey, and that it would end badly.

"Now then," said Grindall, placing the Jocasta back in its pouch, "how am I to find the Tenth City so I can return this treasure to its rightful owner?" His laughter spread over the grove uncontained, then he became quiet before shouting a question at me.

"How do I find the Tenth City?"

I was defeated, my friends were taken, Armon was hours from an encounter with the black swarm. There was nothing left to do but tell Grindall what he wanted to know and hope that somehow Elyon would save us, that somehow he had a way to keep the ogres from defiling the Tenth City and driving him away forever. I pleaded once more with Grindall, just to be sure he couldn't be persuaded.

"If you take these ogres to the Tenth City, they will ruin it. They will drive Elyon away from this place, and Abaddon will rule completely. Are you sure this is what you want? Are you so sure you will remain powerful once he is set free to rule entirely?"

Grindall answered without hesitation.

"I'm quite sure of my place, Alexa. You can stop your worrying about how high and how mighty I will be when this day comes to a close. There is but one way to rid the world of Elyon, and that is to bring evil into his precious Tenth City. It's my *duty* to drive him away. When I do, I'll have power to burn."

He looked at me with such malice I knew then for sure that he was lost forever.

"Go to the Sly Field," I said. "When you get there, take out the Jocasta and follow where it leads you. There you will find the Tenth City."

I'd said it. The secret was out in the open air. There was one last chance, but I couldn't let it show in my voice. Grindall looked down at Warvold, reared back, and kicked him with all his might. I gasped as Warvold went down, watching the blood spill from the side of his head.

"That's for leading me around in circles all these years," said Grindall. Then he looked at his ogres and commanded them: "Gather these prisoners and hold them tight. I'm certain they will want to come along and see their precious Tenth City come to an end."

The ogres all laughed grotesquely, spitting and coughing as they did, until Grindall raised his hand and all was quiet once more.

"Armon!" he yelled. "If you try to break free of our group or make mischief, you'll bring a swift death to your friends here. If you so much as veer a foot away from your leash, Alexa will be the first to go." The ogre that held my waist squeezed his mighty, wet hand tighter. I yelped in pain.

Armon was shaking with anger. Unable to contain himself, he yelled into the air as Grindall laughed and laughed. The forest groaned and swayed at the sound of so much anguish in Armon's voice.

"Now, here's how this is going to work," Grindall continued. "Armon, you'll be tethered to one of my ogres, and that ogre will be tied with a rope to another. If you try anything foolish, Alexa will go first, then Yipes. Take care, last giant. Their fate rests in your hands." Grindall paused, then added a final item, saying it as though it were an afterthought. "Oh, and one more thing, Armon. You'll need to carry old Warvold there, since he appears to be unable to move. We could leave him here to die, but I think I'd rather he woke up at just the right time so he can finally see the Tenth City for himself. And watch me destroy it!"

As Grindall began walking from the grove, I looked at Warvold lying beside me. He wasn't moving, and for a frightening moment I thought he was dead. Armon carefully picked him up and cradled him in his huge arms. Warvold stirred, but only a little. Armon looked at Warvold with great love and compassion, and as an ogre began tying a thick rope around Armon's neck, I was surprised by the expression on Armon's face. He looked at the ogre not with hate but with compassion and sorrow.

Early afternoon was upon the broken forest. We began walking toward the Sly Field in a long line, to places I'd never been and had little hope of ever returning from.

CHAPTER 17

THROUGH THE SLY FIELD

I'd forgotten how swiftly Armon and the ogres could travel. Their strides were so long, like three or four of a grown man's. When they ran, it was amazing how fast they could get from one place to another. It was clear that Grindall wanted to find the Tenth City quickly, before anything else could go wrong. He had fashioned something of a chair that rested on two poles between two ogres. He sat there like a king, high above the rest of us, Odessa at his feet. It looked like a rocky ride, and Grindall often yelled at the ogres to stop being so clumsy. All the while he held the leather pouch around his neck with one hand and ran his other hand along Odessa's thick mane.

Besides Grindall's haste, there was another reason we were moving so fast, a reason I hadn't expected. The grove in the forest was nearer to the Sly Field than I'd imagined it was, and after we managed to make our way beyond the trees and thicket, the Sly Field appeared as if out of thin air. The forest came quickly to an end, and we were all surprised at what we saw.

This was a mythical place, a place where almost no one ever went, and so my expectations were set rather high. I thought there would be fantastic creatures or strange formations shooting out of the ground high into the air. I thought there might be sounds I'd never heard, smells I'd never smelled, and all sorts of wonders I'd never imagined before.

But there were none of these things. An ogre had me held tight to his smelly, moist side, and when he stopped at the edge of the Sly Field I turned my head up and looked out to see —

Nothing. It was as much nothing as I'd ever seen in my entire life. It was flat and brown and barren. And it went on forever. It looked like an endless, dreary desert of hard earth, not a hill or a bump as far as the eye could see. And it was quiet, so quiet that even the ogres held their breath, listening.

Somewhere far in the distance, on the horizon, it was white. But it was so very far away I couldn't be sure what was there, or if there was anything there at all.

As you might imagine, there wasn't any reason to go slowly when there was nothing to trip on or duck under. Armon and the ogres could have run with their eyes shut and managed the terrain. I must admit I was a bit let down by the place. It was nice that it wasn't as dangerous as I thought it would be, but did it have to be so boring and lifeless? I felt about as hopeless as I'd ever felt, dangling at the side of a stinking ogre with my guts being bounced out of me, watching the dead earth race past.

An hour into our journey, I craned my head to see how Yipes, Armon, and Warvold were doing. They were all in front of me, Yipes in the grip of another ogre and Warvold still looking lifeless as Armon carried him across the Sly Field. I heard a sound overhead and craned further still, twisting my body to see what it was. To my great surprise and excitement I saw Squire circling overhead. I hadn't seen her since we'd left the stand of trees near Bridewell, and it was wonderful to see and hear her now. Could it really have only been that morning that I had stood on the other side of the road to Turlock? Things were moving so fast. It felt to me as if all the unseen powers around us were racing to the end of time itself, wanting to get things over with.

I heard Squire screeching in the air once more. Unfortunately, I was not the only one.

"It's that wretched bird," said Grindall. "Stop!"

The whole lot of us came to a halt in the middle of the Sly Field. I looked around in every direction. It was amazing how barren it was, but the white at the distant end was closer now, and I began to think it looked like clouds.

Grindall pulled a bow from beside his chair and set it with an arrow.

"Come on down a little lower, you mangy bucket of feathers," he said, aiming into the air with one eye closed. I looked again at the chair he was seated in. There was a leather compartment that was used to hold the bow and another that held a sword. A third, long and round, held ten or twelve arrows. As I looked at this one, something strange happened.

The arrows began to move around, only a little, but enough that I could tell something was inside the leather container. A moment later, Murphy's head popped out, and he looked right at me. I gasped without thinking . . . causing Grindall to point his arrow down at me.

"What is it, afraid I'm going to pick your friend out of the sky?" He laughed and let the tension off the bow. "Not today, I'm afraid. She's too high, which is where she'd better stay if she doesn't want to be eaten for dinner."

Squire screeched from the safety of the air as Grindall put away the bow and the arrow. I looked back to find Murphy, but he was gone, hiding. I felt sure he was thinking up things he probably shouldn't do.

"What are you waiting for?" barked Grindall. "It's hot, and I want a breeze. Move!"

Armon and the ogres began running again, and I watched as Grindall petted Odessa. It was a miserable sight to see him sitting up there treating my one-time friend like a trusted pet.

As we continued on, I thought about the few hours that remained of the day. If Elyon had told me the truth, my father would be dead in four or five more hours. I could hardly help but feel overcome with grief.

A half hour passed with only the sound of giant feet against dry earth. I hadn't looked up in all that time, and was beginning to fade into a half sleep when Grindall suddenly spoke.

"Stop, you fools!"

When we lurched to a halt, I looked up and saw why Grindall had given his order.

The white in the distance, the white we had all seen, had changed. It had come alive.

My breath caught in my throat as I watched the white mass coming toward us like a flood of water on the land. It looked like a wall of white waves, and I was certain then that the end really had come. There would be no way to outrun the approaching fury before us, and I realized why very few people had entered the Sly Field and lived to tell about it.

"Don't worry about a thing — it's not what it appears to be," came a crackling whisper. At first I thought it was the voice of Elyon, but how could it be with Grindall carrying the last Jocasta? I looked toward the voice and saw Warvold, his head hanging back from Armon's arm, facing me. He'd awoken. I looked at him and smiled, very happy to see that he was still alive. I was afraid if I spoke to him the others might hear, and Grindall might become enraged at our conversation. Warvold continued to stare at me as the white waves grew nearer, coming even faster now.

"What's happening?" yelled Grindall. The ogres were agitated, and they began to stir and back up. I thought they might start to run away, back toward the forest, which would have been a pointless effort.

"Stay where you are!" Grindall commanded. "There's no escaping this thing, whatever it is. If it means to have us, then have us it will."

I kept looking at Warvold, watching him, hoping he wouldn't slip back into his dreams. Even though I trusted him, I was terrified of the white waves bearing down on us.

"Have you tricked me one last time, Warvold?" said Grindall. "Would you really take us all to our deaths just to see me destroyed?"

Grindall turned to the oncoming wrath of waves and laughed, raising his arms as if mocking the power that had come against him.

"There's something I must tell you, Alexa," whispered Warvold, his voice like a thin wisp of air. There was something about his voice that made me pause. With something so big and terrible approaching us, how could I hear such a small voice? It struck me then that the white mass of waves was as quiet as the Sly Field itself — it made no noise at all. It approached as quietly as a snake slithering on the earth, closer and closer. As Warvold shut his eyes and slipped back into unconsciousness, the waves passed over us.

If you can imagine what it feels like to wake from a dream and open your eyes only to see that the world has disappeared, then you can imagine something of what it felt like the moment we were overtaken. Imagine looking at your hand and only being able to see it if you place it a few inches from your face. The world had gone white, with a mist so thick it took my breath away.

"How curious," said Grindall. I could hear his voice, the way he was concerned but happy he hadn't been drowned. Still, the touch of happiness in his voice was gone a moment later as he commanded those around him.

"Armon! If you're thinking of using this development to your advantage, I don't recommend it. Alexa and Yipes are still in the hands of my ogres, and I'd hate to think what would happen to your friends if you attempted something."

"I'm only standing here, the same as everyone else," Armon answered. "I'm wondering what you intend to do, now that we're lost in the Sly Field."

The next minute was silent but for the grunting and shuffling feet of the ogres. During this long silence, something happened that greatly comforted me, something wonderful in the middle of a terrible situation. In the secrecy of the mist I felt something grab hold of my foot, then crawl slowly along my leg until it reached the place around my waist where the ogre had hold of me. There was a tiny flit of a noise, then whatever it was landed on my exposed shoulder, holding tightly with its claws so as not to fall. It was Murphy, come to be close to me once he knew he could not be seen. It made me wonder how he could have found his way in the white that was everywhere. Maybe he had used his sense of smell or could simply see a little better than I could in this strange place. I could see my own hand if I held it in front of my face, and now, as Murphy burrowed in between my arm and my chest, I saw his face and I was happy. He whispered in my ear, but with the Jocasta gone I couldn't understand him. All I heard were the pleasing sounds a squirrel makes.

"Alexa, are you all right?" It was Yipes, risking a question in the mist.

"Quiet! All of you stop your talking. I'm trying to think." It was Grindall, shouting down at us from his unseen chair.

The stone will show you the way.

I thought again about what I'd seen on the cliffs at the sea with Armon and Murphy two days before. The storm had been raging on the water far below, pushing the *Warwick Beacon* out to sea, and we'd witnessed what Elyon had sent us there for. As I hung there on the side of the ogre and reflected on these things, I didn't know what I should do. I'd brought things this far . . . but now they felt out of my hands.

As it turned out, it didn't matter what I thought or what I said. As I was busy with the ideas in my head, the mist began to glow with a brilliant orange light . . . and in that light I saw the wicked face of Grindall staring right at me.

"Ahhhhhhh," he said, "how perfectly marvelous!" He crowed as he held out the Jocasta, then moved it in a circle in the mist around him. The orange light died a

quick death in every direction — every direction but one. As Grindall held the Jocasta in a certain place, the orange light flew out of the stone and illuminated a thin pathway of light ten feet in front of us.

"Go that way! Slowly!" Grindall yelled to the ogres beneath him. They obeyed, and as they went, the pathway of light continued ten feet in front of them. When he moved the light and held it in any other direction, the pathway disappeared and we were lost once more. How I wished I could have the Jocasta back and be rid of this dreadful man and his ogres!

"To the Tenth City, and quickly!" Grindall said, the back of his head a silhouette surrounded by fiery light. We were on the move again, slower now, following a pathway that only showed itself in bits and pieces.

I could only imagine where the path would lead.

CHAPTER 18

THE PATHWAY

Grindall and the ogres had a memory of what the Sly Field looked like before the mist overtook them, and Grindall used this memory to encourage the ogres to continue moving quickly. True, they could only see a few feet in front of them, but there was nothing but flat land in all directions. Going slowly would only bring on the night sooner, and who knew if the Jocasta could provide light through mist and darkness working together against us?

Grindall seemed more agitated the farther we went, barking orders without ceasing, holding the Jocasta out in front of him as far as he could, aiming it just so.

The warmth of the sun had been blotted out, and a moist coolness filled the mist. Murphy shivered in my arms and bore his nose up into my neck as we trudged on. I wondered what he might be thinking. In the past, his little mind was most dangerous at perilous times such as these.

"We're close — I can *feel* it," said Grindall. He commanded his ogres to stop and turned in our direction, holding the Jocasta near his face so we could all see him. He was strange-looking in the mix of light and haze, like an evil spirit come to haunt the Sly Field and live in our nightmares. He held the stone beneath his chin. Shards of light shot up over his face.

"Armon?" he called out.

There was a pause, and for a moment I thought Armon had escaped with Warvold and was hiding somewhere off in the distance. But then he spoke, and I had to admit I was glad to hear him so near to me.

"I am here," said Armon.

"Hand over Warvold to the ogre you're tied to — I have something for you to do." It was a command made with unnerving pleasure. Whatever Grindall was up to, he was acting as though he was about to enjoy something wicked.

"Get one of your own monsters to do your bidding. I'm not letting him go," answered Armon.

The thin light on Grindall's face revealed his changed expression — he was toying with Armon, and he knew who was in control.

"Ogres, give Alexa and Yipes a squeeze, won't you?"

I felt a gigantic arm tighten around my waist and heard the sloshing of the ogre's insides against my head as he laughed. I felt infected by this creature, as though I'd been next to him so long I would never get the smell or the feeling away. Neither Yipes nor I made a sound for a few seconds, trying our best to hold out, but when I felt my ribs about to crack in two I let out a scream that filled the air.

"All right! I'll give him up and do as you say," Armon cried. "Stop what you're doing to them!"

I felt the ogre loosen his hold on me. I could breathe again, but I felt sick. As I gasped for air the smell — the awful wet smell — finally got the better of me, and I threw up. I couldn't really see what I'd done, but now the ogre was laughing as whatever had come out of my mouth ran down his leg and only added to the aroma of death all around me.

"Whichever one of you ogres is tied to Armon, take Warvold from him," said Grindall. I listened as the ogre grunted and laughed.

"You may hold him," said Armon, speaking to the ogre in the thick of the mist. "But if you harm him in any way, you'll have me to answer to." The ogre became quiet, knowing full well that Armon was but a hair away from taking matters into his own hands.

"Have you got him? Have you got Warvold?" asked Grindall.

The ogre grumbled and moaned something, and then Grindall said something that broke my heart.

"Take him over your head and throw him as far as you can. He's dead weight, and he serves no purpose. I don't want him seeing the place he's searched for his whole life, even as I destroy it. Throw him!"

"NO!" Armon, Yipes, and I all cried at the same time. I could tell that Armon was swinging out his arms, trying to grab hold of the ogre. The pressure on my waist tightened again, and I gasped and screamed. I squeezed Murphy tighter than I ought to have and he squirmed free, darting off into the Sly Field to places I could not see.

"Alexa!"

Time stood still in the Sly Field as I heard Warvold's voice call to me, loud and authoritative.

"There's something you must know —"

At that very moment I heard the ogre howl, and though I couldn't see it, I knew that Warvold was flying through the air. I listened and heard the thud as he hit the ground somewhere far away in the white of the Sly Field. I cried out for him, screaming and clawing to be let go from the ogre so I could run into the unknown and find Warvold. My captor laughed while I swung my arms and legs trying to get free, until finally I hung there, sobbing and broken. Would I ever hear what Warvold wanted to tell me, or had his voice been forever silenced?

"So good to have the trash thrown out, don't you think?" said Grindall. I couldn't look up at his hideous face surrounded in burning light and a sea of mist. He was the most awful man I could have imagined, and I only wished that he would go away and leave me and my friends alone.

Armon and Yipes were silent, so silent that I wondered if they were still alive. Maybe Armon's heart had finally been broken entirely, and he'd had enough of our world — and Yipes, he was so small, maybe the ogre that held him had squeezed a little too hard and snapped his insides into pieces. The only thing I did hear that made me realize I wasn't dead myself was the ever-present voice of Victor Grindall.

"Ogres, we are very close to the Tenth City. I can *feel* it. Can you feel it, Armon? You should know. It's your home, isn't it? Don't you wish you could go back there again and get away from all this garbage around you?"

There was no response from Armon, only the heavy breathing of the ogres.

"Answer me!" yelled Grindall. "Don't you want to go home, Armon?"

"The Tenth City is yours, Victor Grindall. You've got what you wanted. Just leave Yipes and Alexa with me and finish what you came here to do." From his voice, it was clear that Armon's spirit had been broken at the thought of having let poor Warvold out of his care.

Grindall laughed and laughed. He laughed so hard I thought he might fall out of his chair.

"To see you falling apart like this is a pleasure I did not expect to enjoy. But what a joy it is!" Grindall proudly summoned his minions. "Onward, ogres! Onward to the Tenth City where we can do some real damage."

And then we were moving again, every

stride of the ogre wrenching my swollen side. Until then I hadn't realized how sore I was. It was as if I had a deep bruise through my entire middle from the pounding, and it was all I could do not to hang there crying.

The next thing I must tell is so very frightening that I hesitate to finish what I've started. I knew when I began this story I would eventually find myself here, in the Sly Field, with my memories of this place so fresh and real. These things happened quickly, without warning, and one on top of the other in such a way that the details are blurred in my mind.

What I remember most is that it started with the sound of bats.

CHAPTER 19

NEARING THE END

"I know that sound, that lovely sound," said Grindall.

We all heard it coming from somewhere beyond the Jocasta-lit pathway. It was the sound of the black swarm, the sea of a thousand bats, and it was directly in front of us.

"They've found it! The bats, they've found the Tenth City! How perfect for me!" Grindall exclaimed. "Now I can add one more to my host of ogres on the way in. Armon, I'm afraid this day is about to go from bad to terrible for you."

"Armon, run! You *must* run away!" I yelled. "Don't let them take you. It's not worth it."

At that very moment I heard a strange sound, a snapping sound, wet and soft.

"Armon? Where are you?" asked Grindall, holding the Jocasta out in front of him to try to see farther. It was a useless effort, as even the sharp light of the Jocasta only lit the ten feet in front of him. We could see Grindall, but he could not see any of us, which gave us certain advantages he hadn't thought of.

I heard the soft, wet snap again — it was a very strange sound — this time followed by a thud on the earth.

"Ogres, I've had enough of this nonsense! Squeeze the life out of Yipes and the girl. The bats will take care of Armon." The black-winged creatures were swarming closer now, not far from Grindall at the front of our group. The ogre that held me laughed hideously and began to squeeze tighter and tighter until I went from feeling pain to feeling nothing at all. And then I heard the sound again. *Snap, squish,* and this time a groan above me. The ogre released his grip around my waist and tumbled to the ground.

I lay breathing next to him, trying to figure out what had happened. I held my arms around my own waist, rocking back and forth, waiting for whatever trouble would find its way to me next. There was a giant hand on my shoulder, and then

Armon's face was suddenly so close I could see his eyes.

"Stay very still," he whispered.

"Where's Yipes?" I whispered back. Armon only had time for two words, but what wonderful words they were.

"He's free."

I shivered as the three snaps I'd heard made sense to me now. Armon had waited just long enough to take the lives of three ogres. First, he'd torn free of the rope that held him and snapped the neck of the ogre he had been tied to. That task complete, he'd managed the same assault on the ogres holding Yipes and me in the mist. Thinking back on it now, I realized that Armon had hours in the Sly Field to observe the ogres and where they were placed in the group, how they lined up. Even when the mist overtook us, the ogres remained in much the same positions as we traveled along. Armon used this knowledge to do what he'd done. I was again stunned at his power.

"Run, ogres! Run into the Tenth City — take it and defile it!" Grindall screamed, knowing things were spinning out of his control. "Follow the sound of the bats and run with all your might!"

Go, I thought. *Run*.

I had to trust in Elyon. I had to believe this was what was meant to happen.

Grindall held the Jocasta out in front of him, and I strained to see what would happen. As I had suspected, Murphy had plans of his own, and he was darting up Grindall's arm toward the last stone. I couldn't see what happened next, but I could guess from Grindall's shattered voice that Murphy was attacking his hand, the hand that held the stone. It flew free in the mist as the ogres charged on, and then I lost sight of it. A moment later there was only the mist all around me, a faint orange glow somewhere at the edge of my sight, and nothing but the sound of bats and ogres and Victor Grindall shouting as they charged into the Tenth City.

Only it wasn't the Tenth City at all.

On they ran and ran, Victor Grindall held high above the rest, the bats leading the way, until all we could hear were their screams as they fell over the edge to the place they all belonged — the home of Abaddon — the great pit at the edge of the sea.

I'd tricked them.

The screams seemed to last forever as we listened to them falling deeper and deeper into the depths. The bats struggled to fly out, but a force greater than their wings was pulling them down, back to their dark source. Their shrieking was the first to fall to nothing. Then the ogres' cries vanished. Finally, even Victor Grindall's terrible voice could be heard no more.

The silence lasted only a moment before the broken world came alive in ways that my memory will never let go of. The land shook violently, and a great, anguished roar charged up from the pit. It echoed through the Sly Field, the force of the voice carried on a thunderous wind that blew out of the darkest places in The Land of Elyon.

Abaddon.

His messengers had been returned to him. He no longer had a hold on our world. His isolation was now complete.

Elyon had won.

A hot wind rushed over me and threw me onto my back, dust sticking in my eyes and pouring over my clothes. I pried open my eyes and saw that the searing wind had blown the mist clear from the land and water, and I was stunned to find we were quite near to the edge of the cliffs. The terrible voice from the pit ceased, and the burning wind accompanying it subsided. At that one moment in time I saw things

I'd only imagined — I saw The Land of Elyon for what it really was.

The clouds that had always hung over the water at the edge of the far cliffs had risen. They were no longer covering everything below. They had risen high into the sky, where they rested in soft clumps. I looked in the far distance and saw bright blue water, vast and beautiful, free of its loneliness at last. The water, no longer hidden from us, seemed almost to dance and sing. But this was only the beginning of what I saw. The rest was even more surprising.

We had arrived at the very edge of the great pit that held Abaddon. It was wide and curved like a snake. Where the pit wall rose up it created a twenty- or thirty-foot ledge before meeting up with the far cliffs that dropped off into the sea. It was on this ledge that Armon and I had stood after swimming to shore from the *Warwick Beacon*. It was the great pit that we had seen, that Armon was drawn to in some terrible way as Abaddon called to him. We'd not seen the Tenth City then, we'd only seen this terrible place, and in seeing it we knew that we would have to find a way to get Grindall to come here. It had been our plan all along to lead Grindall and the ogres to this place and to hope that we could find a way to trick them into thinking it was the Tenth City, to trick them into falling into the great pit.

There was yet more to see, and this last part was the best of all. In that moment, looking at the scene before me, I finally understood how much Elyon loved me — how much he loved all of us. For you see, just beyond the farthest edge of the great pit lay the Tenth City. It was the one place where the mist did not rise completely — it only rose a little, enough for us to see bright lights of every color shooting into the sky and the edges of tall, golden structures. I wish that you could have seen what I saw that day. The Tenth City was positioned at the very edge of the great pit, between its awful darkness and the rest of The Land of Elyon. All this time, as I'd wondered if Elyon had left us or never existed at all, he'd been standing between us and Abaddon, holding the darkest evil back from coming out and flowing over everything.

It was hard to imagine why Elyon had chosen to use me — a lanky girl of twelve when everything began — to finally bring an end to Abaddon, Grindall, and the ogres. He had used the smallest man I'd ever known, a squirrel, and the last of the giants to help him accomplish his plan. I was at once overcome with gratitude that he had chosen to do such a remarkable, dangerous thing. That he would make me feel so important was beyond my understanding.

After the clouds rose into the sky and the mist cleared away, the rumbling of the earth began once more, even fiercer than it had been before. The great pit that sat against the cliffs seemed to stretch itself out. The edge of the cliff that held the great pit to The Land of Elyon crumbled and shook, and then it began to slide down toward the sea. I remember Armon kneeling next to me, holding my shoulder with his huge hand, as we watched the cliff slide all the way down into the water, taking the great pit with it. All of the powers of evil had been contained in that one place — the fallen Seraph Abaddon, Victor Grindall, the last of the ogres, and the black swarm — they were all captured and put to rest.

The water boiled and danced, turning black and frothy, taking with it the great pit and all who were in it. The waves crashed over the stones, and a new cliff was born, this one at the edge of the Tenth City, which stood glowing and perfect before the vast sea.

CHAPTER 20

THE TENTH CITY

It was as though nothing else existed but the sight of the world changing before our eyes. To watch a cliff slide into the sea and witness the Tenth City sitting at the edge of everything was a miracle. I never felt so safe as I did in that moment, when I knew that Elyon would always be there to protect me.

I don't know how much time passed, but finally something happened that seemed to shake the group of us back to life. The hot winds disappeared, and the mist moved back to surround the Tenth City. My first thoughts were of Warvold. He was lying lifeless, alone somewhere behind us, and we were given a clue where when Squire screeched from the air. I looked up and saw that she was flying low, circling in the distance. Her cries were like a funeral song echoing over the Sly Field.

"I'll go back and get him," Armon said. "It will only take me a moment, but I think it's best that I go while the rest of you wait here."

As Armon walked away from us into the Sly Field, I took the Jocasta in my hand, unsure if it still contained the power it once did. It had been in the hands of Victor Grindall — had almost fallen into the great pit — and I feared my time of speaking with the animals was behind me.

For once Murphy was not only speechless, but also as still as a statue as we looked at Odessa standing before us.

"What shall we do to her?" said Yipes, looking at Odessa. "She betrayed us."

I looked in the direction Armon had gone and saw him in the distance, still walking away from us. He and I both knew a secret the rest did not.

"That's not exactly true," I said. "Things are not quite what they seem."

"This sounds interesting," said Yipes, a hopeful look on his face. "Do tell."

"Armon and I knew about the great pit," I explained. "Elyon asked me to bring Grindall and the ogres here, though I didn't know why at the time." I paused, looking toward Armon once more. "It had to be completely believable. If we'd told anyone else, there was a chance Grindall would know we were tricking him. Murphy was with us when we saw the pit, but we didn't even tell him of our plans with Odessa."

"What are you saying?" Yipes was practically hopping out of his pants with anticipation.

"Yipes," I said, "Odessa did not betray us. I asked her to lead Grindall and the ogres to us, to bring them out. If anyone is a hero in all of this, it's her."

Murphy jumped to life, squeaking and carrying on, and then he leaped onto Odessa's back, where he sat proudly. If not for my anxiety over Warvold I might have smiled just then, because I understood what Murphy said. I understood his relief. The power of the Jocasta remained.

I put out my arms, and Odessa walked forward. I hugged her wonderful neck, her fur like a soft pillow against my face.

"Thank you, Odessa. Without you we would have failed."

I pulled back and looked at her full in the face, and she spoke to me with the tilt of her head and a low growl.

"If I had known Grindall would treat me like his pet dog I might not have agreed," she said. "I came very close to biting his hand more than once today. I'm just glad I was able to hold myself back until the very end."

We sat together in the Sly Field, the four of us, and no one spoke. Me, Yipes, Murphy, and Odessa — we were all wondering when Armon would return with Warvold. I wondered if we could have saved him. Everything had happened so fast, but thinking of it now, I felt sure that if Armon had tried to fight Warvold's death, Yipes would have also been killed — and probably me, too.

"There's nothing you or anyone else could have done," said Odessa. "If Armon had fought Grindall, then our loss would have been far greater, and it is very likely that Grindall and the ogres would not have ended up where they did."

Yipes nodded his agreement, and I looked back over my shoulder toward the Tenth City. It was completely covered with white again, and the mist had spread to the very edge of the cliff where it hung like great gobs of cotton on the wind. I turned the last Jocasta in my hand and watched it beat brighter, then softer, back and forth as though it were alive.

My thoughts turned to Pervis and my father. I hoped they were all right, but I had no way of knowing.

The minutes passed until finally we could all see Armon coming back, a body draped across his arms. From a distance it looked like a father carrying a small, sleeping child off to bed, to a place where the child could dream happy dreams. But the closer he got the more Armon looked like the giant he was, and the body he carried looked more lifeless than asleep.

We went toward him then, unable to wait any longer. Squire had lit upon Armon's shoulder, where she seemed to be resting after a long day of flying with no place to land. When we all met at last, Armon knelt down before us and held Warvold where we could see him, and then I saw something I hadn't seen before and I never saw again after. I saw a tear fall from a giant's eye and a bitter sadness so big it nearly broke my heart in two.

"This time there's no tricking death for our old friend," said Armon. "His journey has finally come to an end here in the Sly Field."

I touched Warvold's face and ran my hand along the cloth that covered his arm.

Bring him to me.

It was the voice on the wind, the voice of Elyon.

Bring Warvold home where he belongs.

I held the Jocasta in front of me and realized that it might yet lead us to the Tenth City as Ander had said it would.

"We have one last thing to do," I said. "We must find the Tenth City."

This one statement seemed to shake everyone back to life, determined to bring Warvold to the place he'd sought all his life.

We were up and moving right away, walking the Sly Field toward where we'd seen the edges of the Tenth City in the clouds and the mist.

"Let's not tell anyone about how Warvold came back from the dead and we found him in Castalia," I said, thinking already of all the questions waiting for me back home. "There are those who will say they saw him, but I won't say that. It will be as though his ghost joined us one last time. It will make his life and his death that much more of a mystery, which is just as he would have wanted it."

"That's the thing of legend, Alexa," Yipes said. "And there's no one who ever deserved such a thing more than Thomas Warvold."

It wasn't long before we reached the edge of the mist once more. I held out the

Jocasta and stepped inside. Everyone else followed close behind. As I had hoped, the Jocasta lit a trail in front of me, and I followed it into the depths of this secret place. We were closer than anyone had ever been to the Tenth City, and the earth beneath my feet felt somehow more sacred than that of any of the places I'd walked before.

The mist was darker than it had been, and I realized with a shock why this was. Night was coming in The Land of Elyon. Was it really true that my father would not live through the day? Had I been able to change that? Once the thought had come to me, I couldn't put it out of my mind. I continued leading the way through the mist with slumped shoulders and a downcast spirit. To my great surprise, in the very next step I took, the lighted pathway before me disappeared entirely. Worse still, the light from the Jocasta had gone out completely, and we stood in the darkening mist as lost as we'd ever been.

Throw the stone, Alexa. You can't keep it. It's time for you to give it back to me.

I tried to look back and see my friends in the mist, but I couldn't make out any of them. The deafening silence had come on again, the sound of nothing at all, and everyone seemed to be holding their breath, waiting for me to do as I was told.

"I heard the voice that time, Alexa." It was Murphy, his little voice breaking the cold silence.

"I heard it, too," said Yipes. "And better yet, I heard Murphy just now. How are you, my little friend?"

"Who are you calling 'little'?" said Murphy. "I'm taller than you from where I'm sitting on Odessa."

"Quiet," said Armon. "This is no place for that kind of silly talk."

Armon was not angry — he was awe-struck. This was the place of his birth, a place he never thought he'd see again. It was a place he'd longed for all his life, hoping against all hope that he might find a way back in.

"This may be the last time we speak," I said. I knew that everyone would understand I was talking only to Murphy and Odessa. "I'll miss you both very much. You've been the best sort of friends a girl could hope for."

Odessa crept up next to me, Murphy on her back, and rubbed her big head against my side. Everything that was left to say between us was said in the way the two of them looked at me as only animals can.

"Throw the stone, Alexa," said Murphy. "It's time."

I squeezed the last Jocasta in my hand and felt along its slick surface with my thumb. Then I held it up and threw it into the mist as hard as I could. All of the mist in front of us was blown away, and I saw something that made me very happy.

The Tenth City is not a place that's easy to describe, probably because it's not of this world and there are no words to make it real. The best I can do is try, and hope you understand at least one thing — the Tenth City is where I want to go when I leave The Land of Elyon.

Imagine the most perfect pathway with trees and flowers all along its edge and not a dead thing anywhere. No crusted leaves, no withered branches — even the pathway itself seemed alive with colors. Think of the most beautiful place you've ever seen, and then imagine nothing dead or dying there. Imagine everything in your sight becoming not more dead with time but more alive. The trees, the hills, the fields — all so bright and alive and getting more so right before your very eyes. As I said, it's hard to describe, and I've done a poor job of it. And yet there were things I saw and things that were said that might help you understand a little bit more.

This pathway I've described wound all through the fields of green and gold, bordered by the tall trees swaying in the breeze. Walking up this pathway was John Christopher, looking as happy as I'd ever seen him. As he came closer, I saw that there was no longer a C branded on his forehead, that he was stronger-looking than I'd ever imagined he could be. He was holding the last Jocasta in his hand. Coming to a stop before us, he spoke. His voice was just as I remembered it.

"What a pleasure to see you!" he said. "I only wish I could come out and embrace you all, but I'm afraid this is as far as I can go."

He held out the Jocasta in front of him, and it began to glow once more.

"Thank you for bringing this home," he said. "One day you'll all find your way here as I have, and you will have adventures that make the ones you've had so far seem very small indeed."

I smiled at this thought. It was a wonderful comfort to know that when my life in The Land of Elyon came to an end I wouldn't be lost or destroyed or forgotten — I would begin the *real* adventure.

Armon.

The voice of Elyon came clear.

"Yes?" Armon answered, his voice only a whisper. I turned back and saw that his head was turned down, his face to the ground, holding the crumpled body of Warvold.

You've found your way home.

Armon slowly looked up, and I realized something that made me both sad and happy at the same time. Armon had not only found his lost home, he was *going home*. He was the last of the Seraphs that had become giants through Abaddon's trickery. I imagined that Elyon smiled to think that Armon would provide the companionship he'd hoped for so long ago. Armon was a different sort of creation than I was. He filled some deep need Elyon had for a being more closely like himself.

Armon hesitated, looking down at Warvold in his arms. He was thinking the same thing I was — wouldn't it be wonderful if Armon could carry Warvold's body into the Tenth City? When Armon looked back up again, he let his eyes rest on me, holding my gaze, as if something were about to happen that he wasn't sure how to explain. And then Elyon said something that took my breath away.

Bring Alexa's father with you.

Thinking back on it now, I remember my whole life passing in front of me, the details of my short life streaming through my mind in a haze of thoughts. I thought of all the times I'd sat with Warvold, feeling things for him that I couldn't understand, strong feelings that were more than just friendship. I thought of how alike the two of us were, how he had always treated me like a daughter when I came to Bridewell, how he seemed to have missed me more than he ought to have.

I also thought of Renny — my mother — and of the mother I thought was my own, Laura. These were the same two sisters who had escaped Castalia and hidden in the clock tower where they'd found Armon. And Nicolas — he was my brother, my older brother by a good deal. That explained a lot about my feelings for him. I had always thought him handsome and wonderful, but I'd never felt a girlish crush on him as I thought I should. It was all very hard to imagine, and yet somehow it was as though I'd known all along that Warvold was my father, and there had been a thin veil hanging in my mind between what I thought was true and what I could see. I didn't feel betrayed, which surprised me. I felt something altogether different — I felt complete, whole, and right in a way I'd never experienced before. I felt as though I could finally admit that somehow I was never the person I thought I was, but now that I knew the truth about myself, it was as if I was breathing new air that filled me in all the right ways.

What would I do when I got home? How would I talk with my mother — my two mothers — and the man I thought was my father, not dead after all? It was all very confusing, and yet I was overcome with a feeling of rightness and boldness I'd never known before.

"Don't be angry, Alexa," said Armon. "Your mother and father had to protect you, and this was the only way. Without you The Land of Elyon would have failed."

He looked so perfect, holding Warvold in his arms, his face full of sorrow and uncertainty. He knelt down in front of me, and I walked the three steps that put me close enough to touch my father. Even in death he had a thin smile on his face. I touched his face, tears rolling down my cheeks, and then I hugged him, knowing it would be the only time I would ever see him and know him for who he really was.

"He loved you, Alexa," said Yipes. I

looked back at him, hoping he hadn't been aware of this secret, and in his face I saw that he was as shocked and surprised as I was. All of this had been kept from him as well, and I felt good to know that he hadn't hidden it from me all this time.

Yipes went on, "He never tired of talking about you. Thinking of it now, it seems I should have figured this out on my own long ago."

"I know what you mean," I said. And then I turned to Armon. "I'm not angry, Armon. I'm sad to see you go, and I'm confused, but I'm not angry. Everything is all right."

Armon rested Warvold in his lap, reached over with his one free hand, and pulled me close to him.

"It's time for me to go," he whispered. "My time here has been —" He broke off, overcome with emotion. He looked over my shoulder at Yipes, Odessa, and Murphy, then back at me. "You've been the friends I'd only hoped to find. Thank you for what you've done."

He took hold of Warvold, rose up to his full height, and began walking toward the Tenth City. Yipes, Odessa, and Murphy came alongside me and we huddled together, watching Armon carry Warvold home, to places we couldn't go just yet. Armon passed into the Tenth City and stood beside John Christopher, and when Armon turned around, Warvold was alive once more, his eyes sparkling, looking right at me. Armon set him on his feet, and the three of them — Warvold, John Christopher, and Armon — all smiled the most wonderful smiles. They were home in a place we would all be one day, and I knew then that we would see one another again. I knew then that we would have more, bigger adventures together when it was our time to leave The Land of Elyon.

The mist rolled back over the Tenth City, slowly at first, and then all of a sudden it was gone, and all we could see was white before us.

Abaddon is defeated. It's time for you to go home, Alexa Daley.

The mist stopped short of us, and we stood in the Sly Field as the last of what Elyon had to say to us was said. I knew without trying that my time of talking with Murphy and Odessa and all the other animals was over, and that the voice of Elyon would no longer be audible to me.

"I suppose it's just the four of us now," said Yipes, and Murphy danced around on Odessa's back, squeaking and carrying on.

Squire screeched from the sky above, and I understood what she'd meant to say.

"Make that five," I said to Yipes.

He looked up into the clear blue sky and then back at me. "Let's go home," he said, and the four of us began the long walk across the Sly Field.

CHAPTER 21

TOWARD HOME

We stopped in the night and laid out what little we had of food and comfort, which was a very little indeed. We stared up at the starry night, talking about all the adventures we'd had. The next morning we reached the edge of Fenwick Forest and were relieved to find that it was not as dead as it had been when we'd last seen it. Things were growing — flowers and leaves on the trees. The forest was finding its way back to the way it had once been.

We made our way to the grove and found all the animals I'd met so long ago waiting for us: Beaker the raccoon and Henry the badger; Picardy, the beautiful black bear, who stood with her mate who had returned since the walls had come down; Boone the bobcat, Raymond the fox,

Vesper the woodchuck, Malcolm the rabbit — they were all here to greet us one last time.

Odessa ran forward when she saw her mate, Darius, and her son, Sherwin. It was marvelous to see them together again. Murphy stayed on her back and had some sort of words with Darius, words I was sure Darius could not understand, and then Murphy ran over to my feet and I picked him up.

"Will I ever see you again?" I said. "I think maybe I won't, but that's okay. We've had a good adventure together."

I set him back down, and he looked up at me, his two front feet craning into the air.

"I'll miss you, too," I said, sure of what he'd tried to say to me.

Finally, I looked straight up the grove and saw Ander. Yipes and I walked toward him until we stood only a few feet away. He looked happy to see us, and that was more than any of his words could have given me.

Yipes and I walked on, some of the animals following for a while, until we were alone at the edge of the wood. Home was still a long walk down a dusty road, but we didn't mind. The two of us talked the morning away, enjoying our memories of Warvold and the places we'd been together.

An hour into our walk, we heard horses coming up behind us from a long way off. Looking back toward Bridewell, we saw someone coming toward us at a fast clip. Not long after that, we saw that the cart was driven by James Daley, the man I had thought was my father all my life. Nicolas sat beside him and Pervis Kotcher behind, the three of them looking very excited to see us on the road to Lathbury.

The moment the cart met up with us, James Daley halted the horses and jumped down onto the ground, running to greet me. He bent down on one knee and took me in his arms, and it felt like it always had. He was still my father in many ways, and I still loved him very much.

"You gave us quite a scare, Alexa," he said. "We've been trying to find you ever since Grindall and the ogres left Bridewell."

"We've got quite a story to tell you," I said. "But for now you should know that Warvold is gone, I mean really gone this time." I paused a moment, letting that sink in. Pervis and Nicolas had heard me say it, and they stayed back, quietly contemplating the news.

"Did he say anything to you — anything you might not have expected — before the end?" Father asked.

I took a moment to think this question over, wondering how I should respond. This man had acted as my father when I needed a protector. My true father had always favored this man, and I favored him, too. I didn't want to hurt him now, not after all that he'd already been through.

"I know the secret," I said, and then I whispered, "Does Nicolas know?"

I didn't get a response — just a pained look.

"Father," I said, and he smiled a little, his eyes lighting up. "You're still my father. You always will be."

It was truly how I felt. Warvold had not abandoned me. Instead he had put me in the care of this wonderful man while he stayed close by and made sure I was safe. Warvold was my father, but so was James Daley.

"He knows," Father said. "Nicolas knows."

I walked over to the cart and stared up at Nicolas.

"Why didn't you tell me?" I asked. "All these years you never let on. It makes me feel as though maybe Thomas Warvold favored you over me."

Nicolas stepped down off the cart and put his arm on my shoulder.

"Nothing could be further from the truth," he said. "You were always on his mind. You're all he talked about when it was just he and I. He knew he'd done the right thing. If Victor Grindall had known about you, I'm afraid you'd have been gone a long time ago. And The Land of Elyon would be in much worse shape than it is right now."

We smiled at each other, and I was suddenly very happy to have an older brother. There was a lot to talk about, but now wasn't the time. I felt an overwhelming desire to see Catherine and Laura. With the cart, we could be home quickly.

I sat by my father with Yipes next to me while Pervis and Nicolas took the back end of the cart. There were many questions and much discussion on that ride home to Lathbury, and the hour-long trip passed very quickly. It was odd in a way, this trip home. I was on the same road where it had all begun, only this time there were no walls but the ones around Bridewell and we were going in the opposite direction. As the conversation wound down, I turned to my father and made a request.

"Father?"

"Yes, Alexa."

"Tell me about when the walls were built, won't you?"

"That old legend? You've heard that a million times already."

But he was a storyteller, and this was one of his favorites, so he told it once more, and I loved hearing it more than I ever had before. We arrived in Lathbury just as he was finishing, and I felt a sudden sadness as I realized my adventure was over as well. My heart ached for Murphy, Odessa, John Christopher, Armon, and Warvold, and I wondered if I would ever stop missing them.

We drove through the town and stopped right in front of my little house. I stayed on the cart for a long time while everyone else got off and stood waiting for me. Then the door to my house opened up, and two women stepped out. One was my birth mother, the other the mother who'd raised me. They both looked at me as though they weren't sure how I felt about them. These two sisters, who had held on to the secret for so long in order to make me safe; now they were worried that I might not love them anymore. Sometimes adults can be silly that way.

I came down from the cart and ran to them, embraced them, cried with them until there were no more tears left for anyone. Even Pervis and Yipes were blubbering, which eventually got us all laughing a little and began the process of healing our broken hearts. I had to tell them both that Warvold was gone, and that Armon was gone, too. But I also got to share what I'd seen of the Tenth City, how we'd all be going there someday, and how we would meet up with them again.

I stayed in Lathbury for a while after that, and Yipes stayed with me. We took time to rest and eat lots and lots of food. We mended books just for fun. I took long walks along the cliffs with Catherine and Laura, sometimes the three of us together, other times just with one of them, and we talked about things that are secrets between mothers and daughters. It was breathtaking to look out over the bright blue of the Lonely Sea where once there were only clouds.

Balmoral came to Lathbury a week after our arrival. We had the joy and the sorrow of telling him everything that had happened. He talked of progress in Castalia, and he brought with him the body of John Christopher. When we buried him near the cliffs it helped me to start looking forward rather than back, which was something I needed to begin doing. As exciting, difficult, and memorable as our pasts can be, there comes a time when we have to get on with living.

Almost a year went by, and Yipes never left to go back to his home in the mountains. I think that somehow he and I needed each other more than ever; to be apart would have been too hard. And then one day the two of us looked at each other in a way that we both understood.

"There's adventure to be had out there," said Yipes.

"I know," I replied.

"What would you think of wandering off to Mount Laythen for a spell? You're old enough, you know. They'll let you go. I've heard tales of a strange man who lives in those parts, inventing strange things."

I looked at Yipes for a long time without answering, and then I said something that had been haunting me since we'd returned home.

"I wonder where Roland and the *Warwick Beacon* have gone off to."

It wasn't too long after I said these words that I saw the *Warwick Beacon* on the horizon through my mother's spyglass.

It came to a stop at the bottom of the cliffs, and Roland climbed up the rope that hung there (a rope, by the way, that was hidden well enough and had been put there by James Daley. He had fashioned it with a crank that was surrounded by tall rocks, a crank that Laura had used to hoist up Catherine out of the Lonely Sea when she'd first come home).

The whole town greeted Roland, and Catherine was especially happy to see that he was safe. He was Thomas Warvold's brother, and I think he knew before we told him that Thomas was gone.

"We'll see him again," he said, but he was still very sad to learn of the news. He seemed to age before my eyes at the thought of his brother forever gone from The Land of Elyon.

"Where have you been all this time?" I asked.

Roland just looked out over the sea with a half smile on his face, the wind at the cliff's edge dancing in his hair.

"Home," he said. "Where I was meant to be."

Thomas and Roland Warvold, the two greatest adventurers of our time. One by land and one by sea — and the one by sea was still busy at his adventures.

Roland stayed on for a time, and then Yipes and I began pestering him about his plans. The three of us sat by the cliffs above the *Warwick Beacon* and talked about our future. Then one day Roland decided it was time to go. The town gave him enough provisions to last a very long time and threw him a big farewell party. The farewell party wasn't just for him — it was for Yipes and me, too. After long discussions with Catherine, Laura, and James, I was able to convince them this was what I was meant to do. I'd been home long enough.

And this is where the story I've been telling you finally catches up to where I am now, sitting on the deck of the *Warwick Beacon*, writing down everything so I won't forget it. Yipes and Roland are my companions, and we are on the water somewhere far away from The Land of Elyon. The crisp sea air is salty on my lips and thick in my hair. As I look out in every direction I see nothing but blue water everywhere, and I wonder if there's anything out here to find. I ask Roland the same question I've asked him a hundred times already.

"Roland, is there much out here to discover? Out here on the Lonely Sea?"

Roland is at the wheel, looking very much like the captain he is, and he gives me the same answer he always does.

"More than you can imagine."

I do wonder where this story will lead, if there will be more adventure in this life and what it will be like when I return to the Tenth City someday in the distant future. For now I am content — as you should be — to sit on the deck of a ship at sea with Yipes at my side, not knowing where the story will lead me next.

ABOUT THE AUTHOR

PATRICK CARMAN maintains that he does not now have, nor has he ever possessed, a Jocasta or any other type of gemstone that offers the power of interspecies communication, telepathic or otherwise. Parties interested in obtaining such a stone are well advised to look elsewhere.

Mr. Carman does, however, speak to young people of his own species, sometimes aloud and sometimes in print. He makes his home in the wilderness of eastern Washington and insists that it is a rather ordinary home and is not, in fact, surrounded by stone walls.

Mr. Carman plays no musical instruments, but he has been known to torture dinner guests with attempts on the harmonica. He divides his time between writing, public speaking, spending time with his wife and two daughters, reading, fly-fishing, paragliding and snowboarding.

To learn more about
Patrick Carman and The Land of Elyon
visit:

www.landofelyon.com

The employees of Thorndike Press hope you have enjoyed this Large Print book. All our Thorndike and Wheeler Large Print titles are designed for easy reading, and all our books are made to last. Other Thorndike Press Large Print books are available at your library, through selected bookstores, or directly from us.

For information about titles, please call:

(800) 223-1244

or visit our Web site at:

www.gale.com/thorndike
www.gale.com/wheeler

To share your comments, please write:

Publisher
Thorndike Press
295 Kennedy Memorial Drive
Waterville, ME 04901